UPRIGHT
WOMEN
WANTED

UPRIGHT WOMEN WANTED

SARAH GAILEY

A TOM DOHERTY ASSOCIATES BOOK
NEW YORK

UPRIGHT WOMEN WANTED

Copyright © 2020 by Sarah Gailey

Edited by Ruoxi Chen

A Tor.com Book
Published by Tom Doherty Associates
120 Broadway
New York, NY 10271

www.tor.com

Tor® is a registered trademark of Macmillan Publishing Group, LLC.

Library of Congress Cataloging-in-Publication Data

Names: Gailey, Sarah, author.
Title: Upright women wanted / Sarah Gailey.
Description: First Edition. | New York : A Tom Doherty Associates
Book, 2020. | "A Tor.com Book"—Title page verso.
Identifiers: LCCN 2019042824 (print) | LCCN 2019042825 (ebook) |
ISBN 9781250213587 (hardback) | ISBN 9781250213655 (ebook)
Subjects: LCSH: Arranged marriage—Fiction. | GSAFD: Suspense fiction.
Classification: LCC PS3607.A35943 U67 2020 (print) |
LCC PS3607.A35943 (ebook) | DDC 813/.6—dc23
LC record available at https://lccn.loc.gov/2019042824
LC ebook record available at https://lccn.loc.gov/2019042825

Our books may be purchased in bulk for promotional, educational,
or business use. Please contact your local bookseller or the
Macmillan Corporate and Premium Sales Department
at 1-800-221-7945, extension 5442, or by email at
MacmillanSpecialMarkets@macmillan.com

First Edition: February 2020

Printed in the United States of America

0 9 8 7 6 5 4 3 2 1

To everyone who thought they'd never live this long

UPRIGHT
WOMEN
WANTED

CHAPTER

1

As Esther breathed in the sweet, musty smell of the horse blankets in the back of the Librarians' wagon, she chewed on the I-told-you-so feeling that had overwhelmed her ever since her father had told her the news about Beatriz. She'd known that none of it would come to any good. She'd told Beatriz as much. Tried to tell her, anyway.

But Beatriz never did listen. She always was stubborn, as stubborn as a hot day, the kind that comes too long before a storm breaks, and so she hanged. She swung by her neck while Esther's father, Victor Augustus, made a speech about the dangers of deviance. Silas Whitmour had stood a few feet behind the podium with his fists clenched in his pockets. His lips had been pressed together tight, his eyes on Esther.

Not on Beatriz. He wouldn't hardly look at Beatriz at all.

His eyes were on Esther, who had lied to her father and told him she'd make the whole thing right.

❧

The Head Librarian didn't find Esther Augustus until they were two whole days outside of Valor, Arizona. She swore so loud and colorful that it snapped Esther right out of the Beatriz-dream she'd been having, and by the time Esther was sitting upright, the Head Librarian's revolver was pointed right at her face.

"Don't shoot me," Esther said, her voice raspy. Her mouth tasted foul from two days with only the bottle of water she'd brought, two days without a toothbrush and without food. "Please," she added, because her mother had raised her right and because manners seemed like a good idea when a gun was involved.

"Give me a single good reason." The Head Librarian's badge glittered in the early-morning sun. It was a hammered copper star with three columns etched into it— one for virtue, one for knowledge, and one for patriotism. It shone as bright as Beatriz's eyes had.

Esther wasn't sure if the Head Librarian was asking for a single good reason to shoot or a single good reason not to, but she decided to play her only card.

"My name is Esther Augustus," she said. "My father

is Victor Augustus. He's—he's the Superintendent of the Lower Southwest Territory," she added uncertainly.

The Head Librarian surely knew who Victor Augustus was, but her face didn't change at the sound of his name. Her square jaw was set just the same as it had been, her flinty gray eyes were just as furious, and her finger was still awfully close to the trigger of her six-shooter.

"Leda!" The Head Librarian didn't yell, but her voice carried all the same. After a few seconds, Esther heard unhurried footsteps crunching toward the wagon. The Head Librarian didn't take her eyes off Esther as those footsteps approached, her gaze matching the unblinking eye that was the barrel of her gun. All three of those eyes watched Esther Augustus, and she watched them back, too dehydrated to sweat and unable to draw a full breath.

"Damn it, Bet, if you can't start dealing with scorpions on your own, I'll—*oh.*" A second woman appeared next to the Head Librarian. *Bet,* Leda had called her. The two women couldn't have looked more different. Leda was tall and wide where Bet was somewhere between wiry and scrawny. She was pale where Bet was brown, her skin smooth where Bet's was scarred. Leda's eyes were gentle. At least, they were. Until they landed on Esther's little nest among the saddle blankets and dry goods, that is. When she saw Esther's hiding place, those gentle eyes flashed hard, then went wary and darting.

"Now, Leda," Bet growled, her eyes still on Esther like a snake watching an approaching ankle, "didn't I ask you to check this wagon when we left town?"

Leda didn't answer, but her face told the story well enough: asked to do the task, didn't feel like doing it, said it was done to move things along.

"Please don't shoot me," Esther said, coughing as the words hit her dry throat. "I don't mean any harm, it's just—"

"It's just that you're running away," Bet intoned flatly. "You're running away to join the Librarians."

"Well, I'm not . . . I'm not running *away* from anything," Esther stammered, the lie loose on her tongue. "I'm running *to* something."

"Give the girl some water," Leda muttered to Bet. "She's delirious."

"She's Victor Augustus's daughter," Bet replied.

Leda's eyes got big as she looked back to Esther. Those eyes were canaries, Esther realized—they sang everything that passed through Leda's head, loud and clear enough for anyone to catch. "Shit," she hissed. "We don't have time for this."

"Does your father know where you are right now?"

Bet asked. Esther hesitated, then shook her head. Bet mirrored the movement. "No? Stupid to tell me so," she said. "If he doesn't know you're here, there's not a chance of a consequence for me if I shoot you dead and dump your body in the desert." She sighed, lowering the revolver, and Esther took in a full breath at long last. "Get out of that wagon before you sweat fear-stink all over my horse blankets. Leda, this water is coming out of your supply." With that, Bet walked away and out of sight.

Esther slid out of the wagon on weak legs, her feet slipping in the gravel. She'd worn her most practical shoes, but she could already tell they wouldn't keep her upright on the trails the Librarians rode.

Not that good shoes should be her immediate concern, she thought. She couldn't rightly say that this wasn't going according to *plan*, since there hadn't been much of a plan in the first place, but it certainly wasn't going the way she'd hoped it might. She couldn't think of why a Head Librarian would need to carry a revolver instead of a rifle. A rifle would do just fine for whatever might be in the desert, whatever might come across the horizon to make a woman nervous. A revolver was too close-up for a woman to carry, her father'd always said. A revolver was a man's weapon, made to end an argument.

A Librarian, Esther thought, shouldn't ever have need of arguing. That was the whole point.

A strong, callused hand caught her by the elbow before she could stumble again. It was Leda holding a canteen. Esther would have sworn she could smell the water inside of it. She drank too gratefully, and that strong hand slapped her on the back hard to make her cough up the water she inhaled.

"You don't want to lie to Bet, you understand?" Leda whispered, her mouth close enough to Esther's ear to stir the hair near her temples.

"I wouldn't," Esther replied. She decided not to remember the last time Beatriz had been that close to her ear, the things they'd whispered to each other then.

"I mean it," Leda said. "She'll know if you lie, and if you do, you can forget about her letting you stay."

Esther nodded, her heart pounding. If she played this thing wrong, she had no idea what might happen. Maybe Bet would take her home to face her father's wrath. Maybe Bet would turn her loose in the scrubland to wander, lost and alone. Maybe Bet would pull that iron out again, and maybe this time, she'd use it.

But, Esther reminded herself, that was only if she screwed up.

If she did everything right, on the other hand? Well, then she might just get to become a Librarian.

∽◦∾

A full canteen of water later, Esther was sitting on a rock across from Leda and Bet, and she was lying harder than she ever had before.

"I've always wanted to be a Librarian," she said, looking Bet right in the face, making her eyes wide and earnest the way she did whenever she talked to the Superintendent about the importance of the flag and the troops and the border. Her long hair was matted with sweat in spite of the tight braid she'd bound it in before climbing into the back of the wagon, and she felt like something that had gotten stuck on the tread of a tank, but none of that would matter if she could make herself shine with earnest dedication to the cause. "Ever since I was a little girl, I dreamed of joining an Honorable Brigade of Morally Upright Women, doing Rewarding Work Supporting a Bright Future for—"

"—the Nation's Children," Bet finished flatly. "You memorized the posters."

"I hate those things," Leda muttered, and Bet shot her a sharp look.

"Of course I memorized them," Esther said. If she didn't blink for long enough, she could get her eyes to water a little, so she'd look like she was overcome by passion for the Librarians' work. She clasped her hands together in front of her and let her shoulders rise. "I had one of the recruitment posters hung over my bed since I was a little girl. I love everything about Librarians."

"What's the part that appeals most?" Bet asked.

"I just admire the work you do so much," she gasped, and there it was: her eyes were burning and she knew they'd take on a real shine soon. "Helping to further the spread of correct education is so important. If it weren't for the Librarians, no one would have up-to-date Approved Materials to read and watch and listen to. My father always said"—Bet made a soft sound at this, and Esther reminded herself not to bring up her father again for a little while—"he always said that when boredom takes hold, that's when people get up to trouble. So, I figure that if it weren't for the Librarians, people would probably be coming up with dangerous new materials all the time." She looked down at her feet and gave a soft sniff. "I just want to help. I want to be part of something that's bigger than I am. I want to be a Librarian."

Esther flushed a little with pride. Surely that little speech had done the job.

When she looked back up, Bet didn't seem impressed.

"That was a fine performance," she said, running her finger across the thick, cruel scar that cut through her left eyebrow. "I don't doubt you put a hell of a lot of effort into it. Would you like to try a different tactic, though? Telling the truth, maybe."

Esther glanced at Leda, who gave her an I-told-you-so smile. Her heart pounded hard and fast and high in her chest. That had been her best angle, the speech she'd been practicing for those two overheated days under a pile of saddle blankets.

She stared at Bet, aware that the longer she waited, the more it would be obvious that she was trying to come up with a lie. She closed her eyes and gave her head a little shake.

"Alright," she said. "The truth is, my father was gonna try to marry me off. To a man I don't—I don't love him, I don't even know him, and I couldn't stand it. The idea of becoming his wife, after—" She stopped short, because she couldn't talk about what had happened, not without giving everything away. And she couldn't tell the Librarians all of it. If she did, they'd never let her become one of them. They were some of the most dedicated civil servants on the State payroll— they'd report her for sure.

Bet's eyes flashed. "After what?"

Esther swallowed painfully. *Careful, now.* "My best friend," she said. "She was engaged to him before, but she just . . . she was executed for possession of Unapproved Materials. Some kind of pamphlet about Utah. I didn't know," she added hastily, and it was true. She hadn't known. Beatriz hadn't seen fit to share the Unapproved Materials with her. Hadn't trusted her enough, maybe, or wanted to protect her. No reason could make it less bitter, though, knowing that Beatriz had kept such a huge secret. "I didn't know she had them, or I would have tried to stop her. I would have tried to make it right. I think she was going to tell me, the night before she . . . the night before she was caught. She said she wanted to tell me something, but . . ." Esther trailed off, because nothing good could come of her talking too much about Beatriz. She returned to the better part of that detail, the part she thought would make them like her more. "I never knew she had Unapproved Materials, I swear it. I would have done something if I'd known."

Leda coughed into her fist. Again, Bet shot her a look. "You alright over there?" Bet asked.

"Just fine," Leda said. "Dusty out here, is all."

"So, your friend died," Bet said. "Happens to the best of us. You oughta pick your friends better, maybe."

Rage flared suddenly in Esther's chest and throat,

pounded hot in her temples. "There's no such thing as a better friend than Beatriz, you have no damn idea what you're—" She stopped herself. That wasn't the way to do this. She forced herself to exhale. "You're right," she said, straining to sound calm. "I suppose I should have seen it sooner. I should have been more careful."

Bet leaned her elbows on her knees, stared intensely at Esther. That outburst had caught her attention, it seemed. *Damn.* "So, she hanged," Bet said, her voice suddenly soft. "And you ran off." Esther nodded. It was close enough to true. Bet continued, speaking low and gentle, and as she did, Esther found herself leaning forward, too. "You couldn't stay there anymore, is that right? You didn't want to marry that boy, and you didn't want to stay there if Beatriz wasn't going to be there?"

Her words drew something up out of a deep and locked-up place in Esther's belly, something unplanned and uncareful. "It's not just that I didn't want to stay there," she said, the words coming slow. "I *couldn't* stay there. It was too dangerous for everyone."

"Why was it dangerous?" Bet whispered, her gaze intent. Over her shoulder, Leda had gone very still, but everything that wasn't Bet's eyes seemed far-off as the horizon.

"Because Beatriz died and they were gonna marry me to someone important," Esther said. "I would have had so much power to spread my poison to so many people. So, I thought that if I joined the Librarians . . . no matter what happens to me, at least I'd be able to do some good before the bad finds me."

"Like it found Beatriz?" Bet asked, nodding.

"'Course it found Beatriz." Esther's cheeks were hot again, and it wasn't until she felt a splash on her knee that she realized the heat was from tears, a steady spill of them. She went on whispering to Bet, unable to stop herself, unable to hold back the confession. "We knew it'd find us. People like us, we draw the bad in. There's no good end, not for us. We knew better, we read all the stories—read them too much, probably. We knew that the bad would find us if we didn't . . ." She trailed off, because there was no word for the thing Esther knew she should have done.

She'd talked to Beatriz about it a thousand times, with their legs knocking together as they sat on a porch swing or with their backs in the grass by the creek outside town, or with Beatriz's sweat still stinging her lips. *We have to fix it,* they'd agreed over and over again. *We have to be better. We can't do this anymore.* The last time they'd had that conversation, a week before Beatriz died, Esther had said, *I don't feel that way about you anymore.* A desperate attempt to rescue them both. Saying it had felt like dying, although not as much like dying as the fate she'd feared would come for them.

It was the worst lie she'd ever told, and it hadn't even been enough to save Beatriz.

She struggled to find a way to explain this to Bet, a way to explain how she and Beatriz had brought it all on themselves. "It wasn't that we should've known better," she said at last. "We did know better. I knew better. But I didn't fix it in time, and so Beatriz got hurt. Who knows who else I would have hurt if I hadn't left town?" More tears fell onto her thighs as she thought of her father, her fiancé, her future children. How many people would she have brought down with her if she'd stayed? "There's something inside me that's wrong," she said, "but I thought if I joined the Librarians, maybe I could wash it out. I could learn how to be better from y'all, and then maybe . . . maybe I wouldn't have to hurt anyone, after all."

There was a long silence then, punctuated only by Esther's wet sniffs. Her vision was blurred with hot, relentless tears, tears that she hadn't let herself shed at the hanging. Tears for Beatriz, and tears for herself, too, because the thing she had to do felt so huge and so hard. She would have to dig out the broken part of herself, the part that had made her kiss Beatriz that first time and then every time that came after. She would have to dig it out, and she would have to kill it, and she would have to kill the small secret part of her that loved the broken thing, that had loved the way it felt to tuck Beatriz's hair behind her ears and lick the hollow of her neck and watch her sleep.

Neither of those parts of her could survive, if she was going to keep herself from meeting the tragic end that she knew was promised to people like her.

"I think I understand," Bet said. "You wanted to come and join the Librarians, because we're chaste, and morally upright, and we're loyal to the State no matter what. And because we don't give in to deviant urges. You wanted to come and join us because you wanted to learn how to be like us. Do I have that right?"

Esther nodded, gasping. "Yes," she said. "Please. Please teach me how to be like you." She looked up, wiping her eyes, letting herself have the smallest splinter of hope that Bet wouldn't report her for what she'd confessed. That hope dissolved when she saw the grim set of Bet's jaw. "Please," she whispered one more time, fear tart under her tongue because she knew this was it, this was her last worst hope and this woman who could turn her in to the reaper was looking at her with precisely zero mercy. "I know I'm not supposed to be like this. I want to be like you."

Bet shook her head, then turned away from Esther, her chest hitching. When she turned back, a small, rueful smile was breaking through the grim line of her mouth. She laughed, a laugh she was obviously trying hard but failing to suppress. She reached a hand out to one side, and for one awful moment, Esther was sure that she was waiting for Leda to hand over her revolver—but then, instead of a gun, Leda put her palm over Bet's, and their fingers laced together.

"Well, Esther," Bet said, that irrepressible laugh trying hard to shake her voice, her thumb tracing the back of Leda's. "Well. I've got good news for you, and I've got bad news."

There were three Librarians, including Bet and Leda. The third Librarian was named Cye.

Cye was small and wide-hipped, with rough-hewn features, a crooked nose that looked ready for a fight, and large brown eyes that looked startled no matter what they were pointed at.

Cye wasn't pleased to see Esther at all.

"We can't afford to put her up," Cye said, favoring Esther with a lazy, disdainful stare. "This next pickup will stretch us as thin as we can go. We should just turn her loose and let her make friends with the scrub spiders."

Esther thought that she managed not to make a face at the mention of scrub spiders, whatever those were, but Cye laughed as if she had flinched. It was not a kind laugh.

"We can't afford to lose time taking her back, and we can't afford to go through the Phoenix checkpoint again," Bet said easily, her hands still in her pockets. "Besides, she'll earn her keep. You'll make sure of it." She smiled at Cye, who spat in the dust. "Esther, stick with my Apprentice Librarian here. Cye, show Esther the ropes."

Bet made as if to leave, but Cye made a low noise, something between a growl and a cough. Bet turned back, eyebrows raised, looking something less than patient. "What's got your gullet, Cye?"

"What's the plan here?" Cye asked, widening those big eyes even more. "We're gonna bring *her* with us to collect our parcel?" At the word *her,* Cye hooked a thumb toward Esther, who stood with her arms crossed, trying hard not to take up too much space.

"Yep," Bet replied. She and Cye stared at each other, exchanging the kind of silent negotiation that's based on a thick stack of old arguments. After a moment, Bet sighed. "Yes, Cye. The plan is, we take this one"— another thumb aimed at Esther—"to pick up the parcel. When we deliver it, we'll deliver her, too. She needs to get where that package is going. This isn't up for discussion," she added, and Cye bit off whatever retort had been just under that itching trigger finger.

"Um," Esther said, and although she was quiet about it, Cye and Bet both turned to look at her, sharp as heel spurs. "Where am I going?"

Cye spat again, eye-rolling and knuckle-cracking. Bet shook her head and turned to walk away, aiming her feet at a patch of scrub. She called the answer over her shoulder.

"You're going to Utah, runaway."

Esther blinked at Bet's receding figure. "Utah? That's—that can't be right. That's where the insurrectionists live. Isn't it?" She said *isn't it* as if she wasn't sure, but of course she knew she was right. Everyone knew. Utah, Florida, and Maine—those were the three insurrectionist strongholds, the most dangerous places in the country. Places where the rule of law didn't matter.

"Sure is," Cye growled, glaring hard at Esther. "I don't think it's a good idea for us to take you there. I think you'll just cause trouble, and trouble's the last thing the safe zone needs. But if Bet says you're going, then you're going. And if she says we're getting you there, then you're my problem."

Esther crossed her arms and looked Cye over, the same narrow-eyed up-and-down she'd given Beatriz a hundred times. Beatriz had always described it as her Spoilin' Face, "because that's how I can tell you're spoilin' for a fight." And, Esther reflected, Beatriz wasn't wrong—a fight sounded like just the thing Esther needed. A fight to make her feel less like a fumbling stowaway. A fight to remind her of how brave she was being, running off with the Librarians, leaving behind everything she'd ever known. "Yeah," she said to Cye. "I suppose I am your problem."

Before she'd finished pressing her lips closed around the *m* in *problem,* Cye was right under her nose, a head shorter than she was and a bushel madder. "Then we're going to get a few things straight," Cye said, raising a finger. "You do what Bet and Leda tell you, and you'll get to Utah in one piece." Another finger. "You do what I tell you and you might manage to be something better than deadweight." Another finger. "I'm *they* on the road and *she* in town. You can take time getting used to *they* on the road, but if you forget about *she* when we're in town, you'll have to learn how to think around a bullet."

Esther swallowed hard but didn't blink. She'd kept her poker face on even when she could hear the sound of Beatriz crying under a burlap sack on the gallows. She could keep a poker face now.

And besides—Cye's words sounded angry, but none of them were cruel. Everything they'd said was factual, helpful. "Am I allowed to ask questions?"

Cye crossed their arms. "You'd better. If you pretend you understand when you don't, you'll sink us for sure."

Esther thought she'd gambled right. "Why are you different in town than on the road? Why not just be one thing?"

"Did you ever meet anyone who used *they* instead of *she* or *he*? Or did you only ever read about that in stories?" Cye paused, but not long enough for Esther to reply. "That's what I thought. It's not safe to be *they* in town, no more than it's safe for Bet and Leda to be anything but Librarians who happen to ride together. When there's people around who we don't trust, we let them think we're the kinds of people who are allowed to exist. And the only kind of Librarian that's allowed to exist is one who answers to *she*."

All the fight had gone out of Esther, dried up so fast that she wasn't sure if it had ever been there at all. "I think I understand," she said. "I mean . . . it's not the same. But I had to pretend too." She looked away from Cye, not wanting to see the contempt in those wide brown eyes.

But when she looked back, Cye didn't seem disdainful. They didn't seem as angry as they had before, either. They looked thoughtful. After a moment, they nodded slowly. "Yeah," they said. "I suppose you did."

The silence between them was so uncomfortable as to be painful. Cye wanting to know but not wanting to have to find out. Esther desperate to talk about it but also desperate to never have to talk about it again. Their eyes met, matched, and something grew up between them fast as thunder rolling across horizon-wide miles of sand and scrub—something Esther didn't want to feel ever again. That freckle on Cye's lower lip put a hunger in her, and those rough calluses on Cye's hands put a need in her, and there was nothing for it, and she couldn't look away, couldn't blink, couldn't breathe even, until, mercifully, Leda's voice cut right between them like a hatchet cleaving the arm off a cactus.

"Roll up, roll out!" she called from behind the wagons.

Cye turned their head to one side, not taking their eyes off Esther's, not letting the storm break. "Roll up, roll out!" they called back. "Come on," they said to Esther, their voice soft. "That means it's time for you to get useful."

༺ა

Esther did everything Cye told her to do. She was good at doing what she was told, at being the person she was told to be, and Cye's guidance was easy to follow. Esther thought she wasn't doing too badly, for the most part, although she did use some of the horses' water to douse the coals from the campfire. This earned her an impatient explanation of the ready abundance of sand but nothing worse than that—not the anger she'd been ready to stand up to, not the violence she'd anticipated flinching away from. "We can't go throwing water away," Cye said, rolling up a blanket into a tight coil and strapping it to the side of a saddle. "We smother fire with sand and we wash our dishes with it, too, and we also—you know what?" Cye shook their head. "Just don't do a damn thing with water unless I tell you to do it."

It took an hour to pack up the camp and tack up the horses. It would have taken longer than that without Esther's help. Esther quickly realized that Cye was performing every task with slow, exaggerated movements so she could watch and follow along. They moved economically, their hips square to whatever they were focused on the same way a horse points its ears wherever its eyes are looking. The bones of their wrists were wide and angular, and their forearms were roped with muscle. Esther kept getting distracted by the way the light glinted off the fine hairs on those strong arms. She kept losing herself in the way Cye's fingers worked at knots with quick, clever tenderness, until they gave in at last and came loose.

They were a good teacher, narrating as they worked, telling Esther the names of things and the reasons for them. Esther tightened the girth on Leda's squat black horse's belly as Cye did the same to a leggy chestnut horse that kept reaching back to lip their hair.

"Cinch her up slow," Cye said. "If you go too fast, she'll tense up her belly and you won't be able to get the girth tight enough."

"I read once that you're supposed to smack their bellies to make them exhale, right?" Esther tentatively tapped her mare on the flank, garnering no response whatsoever.

Cye snorted. "You believe everything you read?"

Esther shook her head reflexively, then considered the question. "I guess I do," she said. "I don't read anything that's Unapproved, and I don't think the State would send Approved materials with outright lies in them. I don't mean fiction," she quickly added, seeing the way Cye's face tightened. "I love fiction, but that's not the same as lies. The book I'm thinking of, it was about cars, from back when everyone used to have them. I used to love cars when I was little, and I had this book about them, and—"

"Yeah, I get it," Cye interrupted. "You're bought-in."

"I wouldn't be here if I was bought-in," Esther snapped. "I would be sewing a quilt for my hope chest if I was *bought-in*."

Cye shook their head. "Sure," they said. "You're your own person, an independent spirit, a true outlier. Fine."

They checked Esther's horse over in silence, testing the tension on various straps and buckles. After a few minutes, the tension between them dissolved, and Cye started showing Esther how to braid the horses' manes to keep them from tangling. They demonstrated the braids, explained why they left the tails and forelocks loose, to prevent the horses from getting sunburnt. They left Esther to finish the job of combing and re-braiding all of the horses, imploring her to try to remember anything about them—their names, their breeds, *anything*—by the time she was finished.

But as soon as Cye walked away, everything fell out of Esther's mind save for the repetitive movement of the braiding and the question Cye had left her with. Not the question Cye had asked—*do you believe everything you read?*—but the question they hadn't asked: why *do you believe everything you read?*

༄

Riding wasn't as bad as Esther had feared, once she got the hang of how to settle her bones into the saddle. Her body ached, but in a numb, distant way.

She was riding a horse with the Librarians of the Southwest Territory. She was riding a horse she'd saddled herself, a brown-and-black one that Cye had told her was called a *bay*.

She was far from Silas Whitmour, far from her father

and his constant recitation of the things that were wrong with the world. She was far from memories of Beatriz.

That last part, that was for the best. She hadn't saved anything, hadn't kept a single trophy to remember her by. Not a letter scored with creases, not the locket Beatriz had worn for years and years, not a ticket stub from a show they'd seen together—nothing. She'd left it all behind, and nothing about the scrub or the sand or the gravel or the wheeling hawks overhead did a single thing to remind Esther of their time together. The lizards that sunned themselves on every other stone along the road didn't know about the way Beatriz had chewed on the pad of her thumb when she was thinking. The horse hadn't a single memory of the time Beatriz's parents had gone to another territory for a whole weekend. The desert crows had never heard Beatriz breathing softly in her sleep.

Beatriz was in the past. And maybe, Esther thought, if she was lucky, the things she'd felt for her could be in the past too.

There was, of course, the problem of Leda and Bet. They were clearly together—a couple, and a long-standing one at that. Seeing them together, as comfortable as they were, made it feel almost as though a relationship like theirs might be possible. They had each other, had found each other, and they seemed to love each other relentlessly and fearlessly. It was almost enough to make Esther feel like she and Beatriz could have found the same kind of life if they'd only tried hard enough, only known it was possible, only wanted it enough.

But that was a fool's errand. Esther knew it. She'd seen it for herself when the rope that kept Beatriz from hitting the ground snapped taut.

Esther shook her head and forced herself to concentrate on Cye, who was whispering something to their horse. They leaned in, conspiratorial, and their lips moved in an unknowable rhythm—the horse's ear twitched at the secret, and Esther couldn't help wishing those lips were next to her own ear instead. Cye patted the horse on the shoulder with an open palm as they glanced over their shoulder, their eyes meeting Esther's for a moment.

Those eyes.

Esther shook herself. This was not the time, the place, or the attitude. She dug her heels into her horse's flanks, pulling up next to Cye. Their horse was golden-blond, the same color as Esther's own hair. It was a color Cye had described as *palomino,* and from the glint in their eye when they explained it to her, Esther had a feeling that it was only a matter of time before she had a new nickname.

She was going to force herself to face those glinting

eyes, one way or another. She was going to find a way to look at them without a flush rising in her cheeks, without her hands going clumsy. She had to, she knew she had to—before the broken thing inside of her got out of control and feelings turned into *feelings*.

"Where are we going?" Esther asked, a little breathless from riding. Only from riding, she assured herself. Not from anything—or any*one*—else.

"Pickup," Cye answered curtly.

"Where's the pickup?"

Cye laughed. "Honestly, if you are a spy for the State, you're fucking terrible at it. You're supposed to, you know . . ." Their brow wrinkled as they searched for the right words. "You're supposed to manipulate us into telling you things. You shouldn't just up and *ask*."

"I'm not a spy," Esther said. "I'm just trying to find out where I'm going."

"We're going to the pickup," Cye said. Then, after a moment, they grimaced and added, "I don't know where it is. Only Bet knows where it is. So I'm following her, and you're following me. We've got a town in the meantime— maybe instead of worrying about the pickup, you should worry about how you'll make yourself useful while we're there."

"Do you know how far it is?" Esther asked, and Cye shook their head.

"We ride until we stop," they said. "It'll come before the Sedona checkpoint."

"That's a ways off," Esther ventured.

"Sure would be nice to have *cars* to get there with, wouldn't it?" Cye said, their eyes cutting sideways at her. Esther couldn't tell if she was in on the joke or not.

"Cars wouldn't do much good without fuel to make them go," she said slowly.

"Mm. Well, tell you what," Cye said, and their face softened with private mirth. "While we're in town, you ride on into the Central Corridor and ask the troops if you can have some diesel, and then I'll meet you back here with a car, and then we'll be all set."

Esther laughed. "I don't think they've got it to spare," she said.

Cye nodded. "Sure," they said, their voice cool. "They need all they've got. Can't power tanks with hopes and dreams, now can they?" Esther could tell she'd said something wrong, but before she could ask what it was, Cye gave her a nod. "We'll be at the pickup soon enough, don't you worry. No detours to the Corridor required. Now go on and ride behind the wagons, make sure we don't get any more hopalongs."

After a minute of uncomfortable silence, Esther let her horse slow down enough to fall back behind Cye again. That put her in front of the two mules that were pulling the hitched-together wagons—one of them the wagon where she'd hidden—and behind everyone else. She watched Cye on their palomino, their pace steady enough to lead the two other horses behind them.

The horses Cye had hitched to their own saddle horn by long leads were gray and dappled. Esther had asked what kinds of horses they were, back at camp when she was trying to get everything right. Cye had said "fleabitten," and it had taken Esther a long time to figure out that the answer wasn't a joke. She hadn't figured out that "fleabitten" was a real way to describe a horse until the third time Cye gave her the same answer, with considerably less patience and at a higher volume than the first two times they'd given it.

Esther let herself fall back more, until she was behind the wagons. *Now,* she thought, *we're all in order of importance. Leda and Bet in the front, and then Cye and those fleabitten horses, and then the mules, and then the wagons, and then me.*

The wagon in front held clothes, food, and supplies— that was the one Esther had hidden herself away in those two sweltering days. The back wagon was the more important one, the one with all of the Approved Materials the Librarians were tasked with distributing: books, pamphlets, music, films, and magazines that had been vetted already by the State. The Approved Materials were considered educational and entertaining, honest and inspiring. These were the materials that shaped the nation. They made sure that everyone had the same information, the same stories and the same songs to share, the same videos to watch. They united the entire country, reinforcing the values of the citizens.

Esther had always loved it when the Librarians came to town, because it meant new Approved Materials. Her father was important enough that she got first pick of the things that came off the wagon. She'd never once lacked for new things to read, but she'd still reread the same few titles over and over again: *The Odd Girl*, *Fifth-Story Woman*, *The Lily Path*. She watched the back of the Approved Materials wagon, and she wondered if those stories were in there. Maybe, under that canvas, there were new tales—tales of women who left their husbands, who found forbidden love for a few short days before dying or going insane.

She watched the wagon, and she wondered, wondered hard—until the wagon stopped moving. At the sound of Bet's sharp, two-tone whistle, the mare beneath Esther stopped walking.

Esther waited to be told what to do, why they were stopping. Her eyes were on the back of that wagon, and she wanted to see what was happening, but she'd been told to stay put. Hadn't she? She was so tired from riding in the heat, and she felt sure that Cye had told her to stay where she was. She listened to the distant rhythm of Bet and Leda's voices as they talked to whoever it was they were greeting. The strip of scrubland where they'd stopped didn't look different from the landscape they'd been riding through—that same endless stretch of brown with intermittent patches of green and gray.

Finally, Esther clucked at her horse and leaned hard to one side, trying to peer around the wagon.

There was a shack. It didn't look like a place where a person would live—didn't look big enough to sleep in, even—but it was shade, at least, and Esther couldn't help but long for the cool dark of the interior. Two young girls were crowded together in the doorway, clinging to each other. One of them had the tip of a long braid in her mouth; her eyes were fixed tight on Bet's horse, urgent longing plain in her gaze.

In front of the shack, Bet and Leda were on foot, talking to a man who might have been twenty-five as easily as he might have been sixty. He squinted in the sunlight, his worn face creasing tight around his hard, glinting eyes. He gripped a rifle in one hand. After a few moments of conversation that Esther couldn't quite make out, he let out a loud laugh, his head tipping back to reveal the dark spaces where several of his teeth had once been.

Cye interrupted Esther's view, their horse's hooves crunching in the rough sand. They didn't say anything until they were close enough to touch—close enough to speak without being overheard by any unwelcome ears. They'd changed into a long, dark skirt similar to Bet's, although Esther couldn't fathom when they'd found the time to do it without dismounting. She could feel the heat of their horse's flank against her leg, could hear the creak of leather under Cye's hands as they fidgeted with the reins.

"You're a bookbinder," they said.

At first, Esther thought she'd misheard. "I'm a what? What is this place?"

"Town," Cye replied simply.

"Does it have a name?"

"This is Town," they said again. "You'll see—it's not big enough to have a real name, and that means it's small enough that everyone in it remembers every one of us. We don't need any questions, so Bet and Leda just told the mayor that you're our new bookbinder. If anyone asks, that's who you are. Understand?"

"I . . . what?" Esther said, feeling stupid. "I make books?"

"You fix them," Cye answered. "Supplies are in the Materials wagon, so if anyone asks you any questions, you can just hide in there. You ought to be good at that, oughtn't you?" They started to turn away, as though what they'd said hadn't been made to sting Esther in a tender spot. Then they stopped and turned back, meeting Esther's eyes with a sharp, urgent stare. "And don't forget. While we're in Town, you call me a woman."

Esther swallowed hard, nodding. "Sure," she said. "Yes, I mean. I understand."

They were interrupted by another whistle, although Esther wasn't sure there was much left to say anyway. At the sharp sound, Cye wheeled around and trotted their horse up to the front of the convoy as the wagons started to move again. They stopped so soon that Esther thought they'd forgotten something—but then she realized that this was it.

This was Town.

It was a fistful of dugout houses clenched around a well, everything shored up with corrugated tin and brown brick. There was a hitching post next to the well. Cye and Esther watered the horses there, and before too long, the children of the town had gathered around them. The kids whispered to each other, their eyes fixed on the drinking horses, shy as rock squirrels until Cye invited the girl with the braid in her mouth to come pet one. Once her hand found the horse's flank, the safety was off; the children swarmed Cye, flinging a thousand questions about what the horses ate and what were their names and were they friends with each other and did they have *best* friends.

Esther watched as Cye hauled a little boy up onto the back of the patient mare she'd been riding just a few minutes before, showing him how to grip the saddle horn so he wouldn't fall. They tipped their head back, grinning at the boy, telling him he looked like a real Librarian up there.

"I ain't!" he cried. "Librarians is ladies. I'm a *soldier*!"

Cye's mouth twitched down at the corner, but they didn't argue with the boy. "A soldier you are, then," they said. The boy let out a whoop and leaned forward in the saddle. That mare wasn't about to budge, but Esther could see it plain on his face—he thought he could feel the wind in his hair. He thought he could smell a battle on that nonexistent breeze, and he wanted to go there more than anything.

He wanted to be a soldier for his country. He wanted a chance at a fight.

He wanted a chance to die.

～～

Cye and Esther set up camp a quarter of a mile away from the northmost shack along the road as the Head Librarian and her Assistant went door to door, delivering updated Approved Materials and collecting returns.

Town was small enough that Bet and Leda finished off the Librarians' deliveries well before nightfall; the cookfire was hardly built by the time they returned to the wagons. Both of them carried satchels that hung heavy from their shoulders.

"Doesn't look like you unloaded a single thing from that bag," Esther said. As soon as the words left her mouth, she regretted them—she was sure that she'd said something rude, that Bet and Leda would hear her words as a criticism. But Leda laughed as loud as the mayor of the town had laughed at their arrival.

"We unloaded all of it," she said, taking the satchel off and dropping it at Esther's feet. "This is what we took *back*. Go on," she added, nudging the satchel with her foot. "Take a look."

Esther opened the satchel. There was food inside— jarred preserves, and a cloth bundle that was almost certainly bread, and a glass bottle filled with clear liquid that could only be some kind of homemade liquor. There were also books and pamphlets, all of them crumpled and dirty and as beat-up as a cheating gambler.

"What are these?" Esther asked as Bet dropped her satchel next to Leda's. Cye squatted next to the two bags and started pulling out the food, stacking jars and parcels on the ground.

"Food. They like to thank us, even if we tell them

they don't have to. And kindling," they said, pulling out fistfuls of crumpled pamphlets. There were instructions from the State in there, instructions on useful things like first aid and home remedies and how to defend your household from dangerous ideologies. When they were fresh, those pamphlets were folded into booklets and bound with twine, but now they were worn-out, outdated, little more than trash. The twine was long gone, Esther knew from her own town—pulled apart to use for thread, or wound together to use for rope, or any of a hundred things in between. "We have to take them back, or else these folks would take the paper to insulate their walls and shoes and what-haves," Cye said.

They finished pulling out the pamphlets and the food. Esther stooped to pick up some of the fabric bundles, planning to carry them to the supply wagon, but Cye stopped her. "No, ma'am," they said. The dark fabric of their skirt fluttered as they shoved a satchel with their boot, harder than Leda had nudged it earlier. "You've got work enough in here."

Esther opened the satchel again, realizing that it wasn't empty. There were several tattered books inside, the spines busted and the covers hanging on by threads. "What am I supposed to do with these?" Esther asked, pulling out a book only to have half the pages fall out at her feet.

"You're the bookbinder," Bet said, laying out her bed-roll. Behind her, Leda snorted. "So . . . I suppose you'll just have to bind them."

⁓

An hour later, Leda poked her head into the back of the Materials wagon, climbing up onto the running board to lean past the canvas. "Now, listen here," she said, her voice as stern as the set of her mouth. "You'll have to take to teasing a little better if you want—what in the wide Hell are you doing?"

Esther looked up from her work, her hand frozen in mid-stitch. She held a long, wickedly curved needle between her fingers; a half-dead book on the history of the State was in her lap, the loose pages half-held to the leather cover by a series of narrow stitches. "I'm stitching the pages in," Esther said. "The spine looks like it's been pasted together too many times, and I don't think the paste will hold, so I thought . . ." She trailed off at the incredulous look on Leda's face. "I'm sorry," she said. "Did I ruin it?" She held the book up, trying to see what she'd done wrong. If she'd screwed this one up, she figured she'd have to redo the three books she'd already repaired. Her eyes were tired and her fingers were sore, and she dreaded having to repeat her last hour of work.

Leda shook her head slowly. "You—Hopalong," she sighed. "We were only bustin' your britches. We didn't think you'd actually try to fix anything up on your own." She took one of the books from between Esther's feet, turning it over in her hands. "What'd you do to this one?"

Esther chewed on the inside of her cheek for a moment before answering, trying to decide if she was in trouble or not. "I thinned out some paste and used it to stiff up the fabric inside the cover," she said. "So that crease in the cover won't keep bending and wind up torn. And I patched some of the pages where they were worn thin enough to see through," she added, pointing at the places where pages had been turned again and again, where rough fingers had rubbed away the fibers of the paper.

"Where'd you learn to do this?" Leda asked softly, turning the patched pages and inspecting Esther's work.

Esther shrugged. "I didn't," she said. "I just figured it out. It's not so different from any other kind of mending."

"This is good work," Leda said, putting the repaired book back with its fellows. "Stop for now, though. Cye should show you how a few things are done, so you don't do anything that'll hurt the paper in the long run." She shook her head, hopping off the running board. "Here we all thought you just had to take yourself off to have a tantrum about Cye calling you a bookbinder."

She said it offhandedly, but the comment stung the same way it'd stung when Cye had said that hiding was what Esther was good at. "I'm not useless, you know," Esther muttered, climbing out of the wagon. Close by, the cookfire was starting to gain heat, and she flexed her sore fingers, trying to stretch them out before picking up a knife to prepare dinner.

"Sure," Leda said, not breaking stride. "But you're not a Librarian, either."

Esther didn't reply. She didn't have to, because the only thing that mattered was the word Leda hadn't said.

Yet, Esther thought fiercely. *I'm not a Librarian* yet.

Cye woke Esther when there were still stars scattered throughout the dark sky. "Get up, Hopalong," they hissed, shaking Esther's shoulder.

Esther asked what was going on, but no explanation was forthcoming. They broke camp in silence, Bet and Leda nowhere to be found, and it was only when Cye pulled Esther's horse alongside theirs that Esther came fully awake.

"Cye," she whispered, "is something wrong?"

Cye shook their head, barely visible in the thin light of the oncoming morning. "Pickup," they whispered back.

A few miles past Town, just as a finger of sunlight shot over the horizon, Esther spotted them: six figures by the side of the road, all of them wearing skirts and hats, one of them holding on to a horse. Even from a distance, she recognized two of them as Bet and Leda. They stood in a huddle with four other women, two of them pale and two of them dark. As Cye and Esther drew closer, the horses and wagons behind them, the women turned silently as one to watch their approach.

None of them were holding a package, not that Esther could see. The smaller of the two black women had lush black curls and narrow shoulders; she gripped the reins of a sleek horse that was white with brown patches—a paint, Esther thought, although she wasn't sure if that was a real kind of a horse or just one she'd made up in her head. The woman slipped up into the saddle like a bead of quicksilver sliding across a pane of glass.

Leda held up a hand, still silent. Cye walked the two fleabitten horses over and helped their riders mount them. In all that quiet, the sounds of the horses shifting their weight and blowing at each other seemed like the loudest noises in the world.

The taller of the two black women, the one still on the ground, gripped Bet in a tight embrace. Then, too soon for Esther to decide a single thing about what she'd seen, Bet was on her horse, Leda's fist was lifted high into the air, and they were moving again. The second black woman stayed behind. When she saw Esther looking at her, she made a sharp shooing motion with her hands. Esther realized that she was going to be left behind if she sat around, waiting for answers.

She pushed her horse into a trot—at least, what she thought was a trot, something faster than a walk that bounced her painfully in the saddle. She caught up to Cye and stared ahead at the three new members of their party. The woman on the paint rode between Leda and Bet, her back straight and her carriage easy. Behind her, the two other women—a willowy brunette and a redhead with the extravagant curves of a bull fiddle—rode side by side, their legs stiff in their stirrups.

"What about the package?" Esther finally asked. "Are we still delivering it to Utah?"

"We got the package," Cye hissed at her. "We're going to Utah right now."

"But there's no package," Esther pressed.

"Is too." Cye lifted their chin toward the five women riding in front of them. "You're looking at it."

Esther peered at the women, trying to see what they might be carrying.

Cye snorted. "You must be as simple as you are pretty. They're the package, Esther." They grinned, the corners of their eyes crinkling with a wicked kind of mirth. "We're delivering *them*."

3

Over the course of the next few days, Esther learned exactly how three women on horseback could be considered a package.

She watched them across the fire as she helped Cye cut up jerky for stew. Over the fire, a pot of beans and water and dried tomatoes was just starting to bubble, and the steam from the stew combined with the smoke from the fire to haze the evening air. It put the three women into soft focus, reminding Esther of the Why We Fight reels that always played before Approved films—but these three women weren't young soldiers fighting on foreign soil for the prosperity of the United States.

They were something else entirely.

Genevieve, Trace, and Amity. They were together, *together*-together. A real triad. It was an arrangement Esther had never seen in real life before. She tried to ask Cye questions about it, but they only replied with an impatience that was growing familiar. *Why do you think you've never seen that before? You only ever read about it in stories, right? Why do you think they had to hide in the supply wagon when we rode through the Sedona checkpoint? Why do you think that is?*

Cye only got impatient about questions like those—questions that revealed how many things Esther had *only ever read about in stories.*

Esther had never thought of herself as sheltered before. There was no part of Valor, Arizona, she hadn't walked through. She'd seen poverty and violence. She knew about war and pain and grief. Those last two, she'd known about long before Beatriz hanged—everyone did. Everyone knew about those, and about hunger, and about fear. The country was at war, seemed always to have been at war, and there wasn't a soul in Valor who hadn't lost a loved one, who hadn't gone hungry on reduced rations so the troops could eat. There wasn't a soul in the entire country, as far as Esther could figure, who hadn't at some point eaten an onion for dinner when the meat ran out. Who hadn't fed their babies watery formula, who hadn't learned to make shoes out of worn-down tire rubber.

Who hadn't watched a neighbor hang for "crimes against the State"—an accusation that could mean anything from ration-sharing to assassination to possession of the wrong pamphlet.

But the longer Esther talked to Cye, the more she realized that the list of things she'd never seen before stretched longer than the shadows cast by the desert sun. Not just things she'd never seen—things she'd never known possible.

Things like Bet and Leda huddling under the same blanket next to the fire, a map spread across both of their laps, neither of them looking nervously around to make sure no one saw when their hands touched. Things like Cye's eyes dancing as they spun tales about switching to trousers halfway through a hoedown to spin the half of the room they'd missed while they were wearing a dress. Things like Genevieve and Amity and Trace hiding in the false bottom of the supply wagon as a jovial sheriff with a black-eyed Susan on each hip poked around for contraband.

Things like those same three women fearlessly laughing over a shared flask and talking about the goat farm they wanted to start up in Provo.

Well, no. Genevieve and Trace laughed. Amity didn't. Esther thought at first that she was imagining things, but she started watching Amity closer and found that it was true. Amity's dark curls never bounced with laughter; her warm brown cat-eyes didn't glint once with quiet amusement. She covered her mouth when other people laughed, just the same way anyone else might if they were laughing along, but her face remained still and watchful.

But she didn't seem unhappy. None of them did, even in the moments when they were focused and working, even in the moments when they were angry with each other. Under everything they did, there was a current of satisfaction.

These were people who were happy with themselves. They liked themselves, not in spite of who they were but *because* of who they were. It didn't make sense, not hardly. That kind of joy shouldn't have been an option for women like these ones. It was as lush as a table laid to creaking with ripe fruit and crackle-skinned meat and whole-fat butter. It was a temptation. It was a promise. It was impossible.

She wanted that satisfaction. She wanted it for herself, wanted it like a half-starved alley-rat watching that table through a window on a bellyaching night. She didn't know how to get it—but she had a feeling that if she stuck with the Librarians for long enough, she might be able to figure it out. How to feast instead of starving.

How to like the person who she was instead of fighting it.

"Stop staring," Cye hissed, jabbing Esther in the ribs with their elbow. "Are you finished with that?"

Esther grimaced and handed over the jerky she'd chopped. Cye examined it before dropping it into the stewpot. A few seconds later, the rich smell of the salt and spices the meat had been cured in rose into the air along with the steam from the steadily-boiling beans.

"You did a fine job on that," Cye said, passing Esther a damp rag to clean off her cooking knife. Esther tried to take the rag without letting her fingers touch Cye's. She saw Cye notice the careful way she took the cloth, and before she could flinch away, Cye's hand had closed over hers, rough-skinned and strong. They gave her knuckles a squeeze before letting go, and the ghost of smile lifted the corners of their mouth. "Cut it up evener than I did."

Esther's breath was stuck somewhere south of her tongue. She looked away sharp, pulling her hand away from Cye's, taking the rag with it. "I'm good in the kitchen," she said, her voice as near to steady as she could get it. "My mother, she thought it was important . . . she wanted to make sure I knew how to do things the right way."

She found herself stumbling over the words. Her mother taught her the things that a girl should know—managing household finances, cooking and hosting, sewing, cooking with rations. She'd always been patient, kind, generous, tender.

She'd done as well as Esther supposed anyone could have.

But she'd also never stepped in when Esther's father was cruel for cruelty's sake. She'd never stopped him from being the kind of man who had to apologize in the morning for what he'd said and done the night before. She taught Esther how to hide bruises, but she'd never done a thing to prevent them.

She'd always said that it was just the way of things. *He's our leader,* Esther's mother had said. *He gets to decide how he wants to lead.*

Esther never knew if her mother believed those words, or if they were just something she told herself to make up for the fact that there wasn't a thing to be done about him. Victor Augustus was powerful, but even if he hadn't been powerful, he had the right to run his household as he saw fit. Esther didn't know that she could forgive the way her mother had raised her, but she could understand it.

And, she thought bitterly, at least she knew how to dice meat for stew.

"I think that knife's about clean," Cye drawled, and Esther realized she'd been lost in thought, scrubbing her cooking knife with the damp rag for so long that it was a wonder the blade hadn't sawed right through the cloth. She folded the rag carefully, rested the knife on it.

"Sorry," she said. "Distracted, I guess. It's been some kind of a day."

Cye let out a sharp laugh. "Tell me about it. When you showed up, I thought I'd have to watch a hopalong get dragged out into the desert to wander, and instead I got promoted to chief babysitter. Didn't know how much extra work you'd be."

Esther winced. "I'm not a kid. You don't have to babysit me."

"You might as well be a kid," Cye said, not unkindly. "You know as much about living out here as a three-year-old knows about drone repair. I just hope you can learn as fast as a toddler would."

The fire let out a sharp *crack,* and a log spit sparks high into the air. For a brief moment, Cye's face was thrown into deep shadow.

Esther cleared her throat. "What, uh—what quadrant are you from?"

"Low Northeast." From the way Cye answered, it was clear that they knew what question they were really answering: *what did you do?* There was no formal division of purpose between the quadrants, except for the Central Corridor, but there were practical divisions. The Northeast quadrant was thick with factories, and those factories needed the nimble fingers of small children who could manage military circuitry with precision.

Esther would have wagered that Cye knew exactly how fast a toddler could learn to repair a busted drone.

Her eyes landed on the other women across the fire. Bet and Leda were still tucked under the same saddle blanket. Leda was resting her head on Bet's shoulder, her eyes on the fire. Bet's lips were moving, saying something soft that made Leda wrinkle her nose.

Cye poked at the fire with a stick. "Before you ask, I'll answer." They spoke in a low, soft voice that didn't carry to anyone's ears but Esther's. "Leda's from the Northwest. Last name used to be Proud, but she doesn't use it anymore and you'd do well never to use that word in her hearing, no matter what you mean by it. Nod if you understand, you're too loud a talker to answer."

Esther nodded—she'd heard of the Proud family, an organized crime syndicate founded on bloodshed and terrorism. They had once controlled a large swath of the Northwest. Every time her father had hosted a guest from up that way, they seemed embarrassed that the Proud family still existed.

Cye nodded back, then added, "Bet's from the Central Corridor."

Esther's brow furrowed. "From—"

"Yep," Cye cut her off before she could finish asking.

"But nobody's *from* the Central Corridor," Esther whispered, irritated at Cye's haughty shrug.

"Not everyone who lives there's a soldier," Cye said. "People just think that because no one ever leaves the CC without doing a tour of combat first. But kids grow up there, sure. And I guess Bet didn't want to fight just because somebody told her she had to."

Esther scoffed. "Women can't go to combat, we have to stay domestic to tend the homestead. She could have just stayed—"

"Anyway," Cye interrupted. "Don't ask her about the CC. Don't ask Leda about the Northwest. We all come from somewhere, and none of it is secret or else I wouldn't tell you, but . . ." They sighed, their shoulders drooping, and Esther realized that they must be twice as tired as she was. "But it's not great to talk about. We all had reasons for leaving home and joining the Librarians, you know? Nobody wants to relive those reasons." Their lips twitched into an insufferable smirk. Esther realized how much she had been watching their mouth as they talked, the way they bit their lower lip and ran their tongue across their teeth—slow and purposeful, just the way they were now. "Unless," they added, "you want to talk about why *you* left home. Girl trouble?"

Esther coughed, choking on nothing at all, and Cye's smirk grew into an actual smile. They had dimples.

Deep ones.

"No, nothing I want to talk about," Esther snapped, trying to get mad enough to stop noticing how those dimples deepen. She watched Cye stretch forward to stir the stew, their sinewy arm lit from below by the flickering fire. They glanced over their shoulder at her, their eyes wicked and knowing, and she felt herself flush the kind of deep red that had always made Beatriz erupt in throaty laughter.

She fought it back. It felt like a betrayal of the life she was trying to build here. It felt like a betrayal of Beatriz, of what they'd been to each other.

"You're staring again," Cye murmured, sitting back onto their bedroll. They stretched their legs out in front of them, balancing the heel of one boot on the toe of the other. The button fly of their jeans glinted in the firelight. "Penny for your thoughts?"

Esther would have charged a great deal more than a penny for the kinds of thoughts that entered her mind at the way Cye looked up at the stars—at the way their shoulders strained at their shirt, at the way the long expanse of their throat opened to the sky, at the way their ropy muscles made their freckle-dusted arms taut. She swallowed hard, pinched her arm to try to get those thoughts to go back where they belonged. "I was thinking about the stew," she lied. "I was thinking about the jerky. It's clever."

"Sure," Cye said, casting Esther a sidelong glance that said *I know* that's *not what's on your mind.* "It softens up real nice, gives the stew a good flavor. And we need the protein. We work hard. Beans aren't quite enough fuel, not out here."

Esther chewed on her lower lip, staring at the fire so she wouldn't stare at Cye. "You know," she said, "we could put a little wine in that stew. Or if we could get a jar of whole tomatoes, or even vinegar—"

"What?" Cye snapped. "Why? It tastes fine with the dry tomatoes."

Esther cleared her throat. "Sure," she said. "I'm sure it does. But some acid in there would make the meat get soft faster, so you could eat sooner. And the meat would be more tender."

"We try not to carry glass in the wagons." Leda's voice carried from across the fire, and Esther realized that everyone had been listening to her. "We can't guarantee that bottles of anything would stay intact, not when the road gets rough."

"But we could get wine in synth-pouches," Bet said slowly. "Or a small barrel of beer. Would that work the same, Esther?"

Esther felt cornered. She felt certain that she'd done something wrong, that she'd stepped out of line. She wasn't used to speaking out of turn, wasn't used to sharing her ideas out loud when she hadn't been told to. "I'm— Maybe? I've made stew with beer before, so I suppose it might work?" Everyone was staring at her, interested and intent. "What? Why are you all looking at me?"

"Because you're being interesting," Amity said. It was the first time Esther had heard Amity speak. Her voice was disarmingly high, light and lilting. "You know how to cook?"

"Sure," Esther said, trailing off before she could start stammering about her mother again.

"We'll see what we can see," Bet announced. "We'll be in town tomorrow for some supplies. I'll also put your stew ingredients on the list, and we'll find out if they do what you say they will. If they're not too much trouble, we can add them to the regular rotation. You're on dinner duty tomorrow night. Goes well enough? Well, then I expect we'll know what to do with you until we get where we're going."

With that, Bet returned her attention to whatever she'd been telling Leda before. The conversation was over. Esther couldn't tell if she'd done something wrong or if she'd done something right. She shared an uncertain glance with Genevieve and Trace, both of whom had watched this exchange with wide, wary eyes; they offered her no answers.

Neither did Cye. "We'll just have to see, Hopalong," they murmured, giving the stew a last stir before beginning to ladle it into tin mugs. They shook their head ruefully, squinting against the smoke, not looking at Esther. "We'll just have to see what you can do."

CHAPTER

4

Leda and Bet left camp just before dawn, leaving Cye in charge. They rode off to the east, and Esther watched them until the dust clouds their horses kicked up were the only evidence of them she could spot. It wasn't long before even that faded into the dull gray of the sunless desert.

"Cold?" Cye tossed a blanket at Esther without looking at her.

Esther hesitated, gripping the rough weave of the blanket between her fists. "No," she said. "I'm fine. I don't really notice the cold."

Cye snorted. "You're shivering. Wrap up already, will you? There's no prizes for being impervious out here."

"The cold is helping me wake up," Esther insisted.

"It ain't," Cye said, their voice easy but authoritative. "You think it is, but really, it's just gonna wear you out more." They moved a few paces closer to Esther, their boots crunching softly in the gravel. The quiet of the early morning seemed to amplify every sound, and Esther could hear their every breath before she saw it puff out into a cloud in front of their mouth. "You stand there shivering, thinking you're awake, but you're using up all your energy to try to stay warm." A few more steps, and then they were right in front of her, their wide-set brown eyes serious. "And then later, once you get warm, you're more tired than ever." They gently tugged the blanket out of Esther's hands. Their callused fingers brushed hers. An electric thrill ran up her spine, and she shivered once, hard. Cye's lips tightened as if they were fighting a smile. "Here," they said, and they reached around Esther's shoulders to wrap her up in the blanket. "Trust me. This is better than pretending you're not cold."

Esther was quite a bit warmer already than she had been when Cye first flung the blanket at her. "Thank you," she whispered. Cye was so close to her that the mist of her breath brushed their throat. They were still holding the blanket closed around her. "I'll keep that in mind," she added.

"Good," Cye murmured.

"Good," Esther said back, echoing Cye's words automatically because she didn't know what else to say, because *you have a freckle on your bottom lip* seemed like the wrong thing to say but it was the only thing she could think.

At least, it was the only thing she could think until another thought stepped in to join it, an even more unwelcome one. *What would Beatriz think if she were here?*

Of course, Esther knew exactly what Beatriz would have thought, what she would have said. She would have been merciless, teasing and poking at Esther, telling her to hurry up and make a move already, long before Esther could even think about what *making a move* could mean. She would have been spinning elaborate fantasies of what Cye and Esther could become to each other, of a future they could have, regardless of whether Esther wanted that future.

Relentlessly unpossessive, that was Beatriz. Wild with it. The only thing she'd ever seemed attached to was the idea that none of it mattered.

Esther had tried to learn how to believe that same thing, that none of it mattered. She'd tried her best.

Amity emerged from the tent she shared with Genevieve and Trace, stretching. Her yawn was a little too theatrical to be convincing, and Esther felt certain that she'd been eavesdropping on their conversation, waiting for the right moment to ruin it.

No, Esther corrected herself. *Amity was waiting for the right moment to rescue me from myself. I'm glad she interrupted us. I'm thankful.*

"Morning," Amity drawled. "Any chance either of you could use a hand getting that fire going?"

"I think Esther can handle it," Cye replied with a lightning-fast wink. "Y'all feel free to take it slow this morning. Bet and Leda won't be back until noon, so we've got a lazy morning in front of us. Well," they corrected themselves, "you three've got a lazy morning in front of you, at least."

"Never was one for sleepin' in." Amity wandered past Esther to poke at the embers of last night's fire. Either she hadn't heard Cye say that Esther could handle the fire, or she didn't believe it was true. Regardless, Esther was grateful for her intervention. She watched closely as Amity prodded the embers closer to each other.

"You watch more than you talk," Amity murmured. "Fetch me my whittling bag." Esther grabbed the small linen bag Amity had left near the fire the night before. "See?" Amity chuckled. "Most people would ask 'where is it,' or 'which bag should I look for,' or 'why.' Not you, though. Doesn't occur to you to pretend like you don't watch people."

"I'm just trying to learn," Esther said.

Amity laughed. "I just bet you are." She reached into the bag and pulled out a fistful of wood shavings, tossing them onto the embers. They began to curl, fragrant, the smoke they put off catching a few beams of early sunlight. Amity built the fire up in silence, adding more kindling and then a few small logs. By the time they were burning steadily, Cye had returned with a pot of water.

"In case you want coffee," they said, handing over the pot. "Tomorrow, Esther, you're in charge of the morning fire. Understand? Don't be making our guests do your chores for you."

Before Esther had time to object, Amity was handing the water back to Cye, her eyes on the desert behind them. "No coffee today, I'm afraid. Don't reckon we'll have time for it," she said, shaking her head. "Saddle up. We've got ten minutes at the outside, I'd say closer to six to be safe."

"What?" Cye looked down at the pot of water in their hands as though it might know what the hell Amity was talking about. "What are you—wait!" They handed the water to Esther and followed after Amity, who was already jogging back toward her tent. "Where are you going?"

"Waking up my people," Amity called over her shoulder, her dark curls bouncing hard as she ran. "You'd best get yourselves together. Company's coming." She stuck her head into her tent, and the muffled sounds of her waking her bedfellows came soon after.

"What's she talking about?" Cye muttered, looking around. "I don't—"

"There," Esther interrupted, because she finally saw what Amity had seen, and it wasn't good. "She's right, Cye. We should get some horses ready, or at least the wagons. If, I mean—if that's alright with you—"

"Will you quit hemming your petticoats and tell me what in the hell it is you think is going on here?" Cye snapped, fury quickly building in their voice.

Rather than answer, Esther pointed to the horizon. She stepped around Cye, keeping her finger aimed at the same spot of desert as she moved so they could sight along her arm and see what she saw, what Amity had seen.

A growing cloud of dust coming from the east, near impossible to see, thanks to the blinding light of the rising sun creeping over the horizon. The only reason that dust cloud was visible at all was because it was bigger than just two horses could ever hope to kick up, and moving faster than fast.

It was moving right toward the Librarians' camp.

"Shit," they spat. "That's trouble, alright. Go tack up the horses. You won't be able to do them all before that mess arrives, but do what you can. Go, quick now, you remember how to do it."

Esther ran to the horses, her shoes sliding out from

underneath her. By the time she got the saddle fixed on Cye's palomino, the sound of hoofbeats was just barely audible—but it wasn't quite enough to cover the sound of conversation from the camp.

"I'll handle the package." That was Amity's voice, brusque and direct.

"I don't think so." That was Cye, breathless. Their next words were drowned out by one of the fleabitten horses—Esther couldn't tell them apart—whickering for attention.

"Trust me." Amity again. "Here, wear this."

Cye's voice bled *we don't have time for this*. "I'm in charge here, and—"

"You're in charge here, and we're liabilities, sure. But we can be our own problem for the time being. Now, trust me with these two ladies and handle your business."

There was a flurry of swearing and scuffling, and then Cye came stumbling over, one leg in a skirt and the other leg out of it. The sound of hoofbeats was closer now, punctuated by shouting.

"You almost finished?" Cye snapped, yanking the skirt on right over their pants and furiously tucking their shirt into it.

"Near about," Esther replied, although she had no idea how to make the damn horse open its mouth. She got close, thought the horse was about to succumb—but then a loud *pop* cut through the air. The horse jerked its head away, and Cye's face lost a shade of color.

"Was that . . . ?" Esther started to ask, and Cye gave a quick, jerky nod.

"Gunfire," they confirmed. "C'mon and leave that be, two horses is enough for us. Amity'll handle it if those three need to ride off." They hesitated. "Maybe . . . maybe it'd be better for them if it seems like there's just the two of us." Cye froze, staring at the bridle on the half-tacked gray horse in front of Esther. The whites of their eyes seemed too bright in the early-morning light. They didn't blink until those *pop*s sounded again, louder this time. Closer. "Fuck," they whispered. "I don't—I don't know—"

"Leave it," Esther said, grabbing Cye by the arm. "I don't think it's going to make much difference."

Cye glared at her for a moment before nodding and lacing their fingers together in a low sling. "Hop up then," they said. "It's time to ride."

Esther planted her foot in their hand, grabbed the saddle, and swung herself up onto the back of the same bay horse she'd been riding. She thought she was getting the hang of horses. After just a few moments of scrambling, she was settled in the saddle and ready to ride.

"We go south," Cye said, pointing their palomino

back the way they'd come the day before. "They'll chase us, and that'll give Amity time to get the camp tucked away so there's nothing to find here if they're the kinds of people who'd look for it. Keep riding until we lose them or they find us. If they find us, we're sisters, on our way to a wedding, and we rode off fast because we got scared. If they find us, you call me a girl no matter what." They looked at Esther so intensely that she felt certain they'd be shaking her if they could only reach her. "No matter what. Got it?"

Soon as Esther nodded, they gripped their horse's reins in one hand and planted the other atop their hat. But before they could ride away in their own cloud of dust, a piercing whistle rose over the pops of gunfire and the sounds of hoofbeats.

It was a damn familiar whistle.

Cye's head snapped to the east, toward that whistle, the light of the rising sun casting deep shadows across their face. "Leda?" they whispered. The whistle sounded again, and they swore again. "Change of plans," they said. They hiked their skirt up, tucking it into their waistband, out of the way of their legs. A quick fumble underneath it, and then they had a short-nosed revolver in their hand. "Follow me."

With that, they wheeled their horse around and shouted, leaning forward in their saddle. The palomino reared back, letting loose a shrill whinny. Cye shouted again, and the palomino took off.

It headed directly toward the oncoming hoofbeats. And before Esther could register what was happening, her own horse shook its head and began to follow.

"No, no no no, I don't—" Esther tried to remember the word Cye had told her meant "stop" to a horse. "Whoa? *Whoa!*" She tried that one, the only thing she could remember, and she yanked hard on the reins, but the horse underneath her might as well have been a runaway freight train for all she could get it to slow down. It pulled up next to Cye, and the sound of hoofbeats was right on top of them, and then they were in the fray.

Choking dust flew up around them. The sound of gunfire was impossible to trace—it could have been coming from anywhere, seemed to come from everywhere. Esther looked, frantic, trying to spot Bet or Leda, trying to see what was going on. That piercing whistle came again, from right behind Esther this time, and when she twisted in her saddle, there was Leda, with Bet close behind.

"Bandits!" Leda shouted. Sure enough, Esther looked around her again and saw what she'd missed in the chaos of men and horses: everyone who wasn't her or Cye or Leda or Bet was wearing a black bandana over his nose and mouth. They were men, all of them, angry-eyed in a way Esther hadn't seen since she'd looked down at the crowd that had surrounded Beatriz's gallows. "Esther, can you shoot?"

Esther shook her head, then realized there wasn't a chance in hell Leda had seen the gesture. "No," she yelled back. "What can I do?"

Bet lifted an arm in the air and swung it in a tight circle. "Keep 'em flustered!" she yelled. "I already took two down, there's just four left to go!"

The confusion of the fight was intense and inescapable. Esther was overcome with a sharp, intent focus. She rode between the bandits, driving them in unexpected directions and distracting their horses as Bet, Leda, and Cye picked them off with well-aimed gunshots. Esther had no idea what direction she was riding in, no idea how long the fight was taking. Bullets flew all around her, and some of them must have been flying at her, but there wasn't time to wonder which was which, because all of them were coming too close to her by miles. She rode so close to the bandits that their horses' mouths left flecks of foam on her skirts, and every moment felt like it was going to be the moment where everything went wrong, the moment where she'd wind up on her back in the dust with a hoof on her throat.

She was so afraid, but there was no time for her to think about how afraid she was. All she knew was that she needed to get out of the way of the Librarians, and at the same time she needed to get *in* the way of the bandits, and every single second that passed contained a thousand different decisions all at the same time.

Finally, there was one bandit left. His black bandana was tight over his nose and mouth, leaving only a pair of thick white eyebrows exposed. He was pink-faced and furious, sweating hard. His wild-eyed stallion was just as lathered as he was, and the horse was beginning to slow down in spite of the frantic way his rider lashed the reins at his left and right flanks.

As the bandit lashed at the right flank, the Librarians approached him from all sides.

As he lashed at the left flank, Bet's horse shied away from his, trying to avoid those flailing reins.

As he lashed at the right flank again, Esther galloped up beside him. And as he swung his reins around again to try to lash his horse on the left, Esther reached her hand out.

She caught the reins. Her shoulder jerked with an agonizing pop, and white-hot pain flashed through her arm and across her back, but she gripped the leather tight and didn't let go. The bandit looked at her, his eyes wild with fury, jerking at the reins with one hand and aiming his gun with the other.

Behind him, Bet managed to get her horse back in

line. She nodded to Esther and shouted something unintelligible, and Esther could only hope that she was reading that signal right, because she knew that there would be no second chances this time.

The bandit cocked the hammer of his thumb-buster and gave the reins a final, vicious yank.

Esther let go.

The bandit overbalanced, fumbling his gun. The unmistakable sound of a final gunshot rang out loud over the noise of the horses—and with that, it was over.

The bandit drooped forward over his saddle, his spine going as limp as laundry.

With his body out of the way, Esther could see Bet's revolver, still pointing at the place where he had been.

"Well," Bet said breathlessly as the horses began to slow. "Well." Beside her, the bandit's blood ran freely across the heaving, lathered flanks of his stallion. Bet holstered her gun, then leaned sideways to gently take the stallion's reins. He matched the pace set by her mare, and soon, the horses were walking instead of running— Bet and Esther flanking the stallion, with Leda in front of them and Cye behind.

"Well," Bet said once more, wiping her forehead before looking up at Esther with a hopeful smile. "This horse is a good get, but he's damn well baked from that run, and so am I. I don't suppose y'all made coffee before you came out to meet us, did you?"

"No," Esther managed after a moment. "We got distracted by the, uh. By the run."

Bet let her own horse's reins drop and used her free hand to fan herself with her hat. "Damn," she said. "No hard feelings, but I could use a cup of coffee about now. Never you mind—we'll just have to get on back to camp and make a pot." Esther looked up at the direction they were headed, trying to get her bearings. She could just make out the shape of the wagons in the distance. As she watched, Bet replaced her hat and gave her mare a friendly slap on the shoulder. "Would have been cold by the time we got back, anyway," she muttered.

"We'll get you some soon's we get settled again," Cye called from behind them. "Don't worry about it. Esther?"

"Yeah?" Esther called back, trying hard to understand how it was possible that they were talking about coffee.

When Cye answered, it was with barely restrained laughter. "You're in charge of relighting that fire."

CHAPTER

5

The Librarians had a problem. It was a big problem, a problem that seemed to take up the entire camp even though it only had the footprint of a laid-out bedroll.

Amity dug a booted toe into the ribs of that big problem and shoved. The big problem didn't do anything about it, on account of being dead.

"That's the sheriff from Sedona," Amity said.

"Yeah, we figured that out while you were fetching Gen and Trace back from whatever snakehole you all found to hide in," Bet replied, standing next to Amity with her arms folded across her chest.

"Why would he be with a gang of bandits?" Esther muttered. She couldn't stop staring at the dead man. She'd had a hand in his death—in the deaths of all his compatriots, too, sure, but them, she'd only distracted. This man, she'd held in place. She'd grabbed his horse by the reins and kept him still long enough for Bet to part his hair with a bullet.

He was bleeding on her bedroll, and he was doing it because she'd ridden a horse the right way to put him there.

"That must've been his posse," Leda murmured. "Only difference between a sheriff's posse and a gang of bandits is a man with a star pinned on his shirt."

"He protects Sedona, doesn't he?" Esther asked, trying not to sound naive and hearing herself fail at it. "I mean, won't he be missed there?"

"He keeps Sedona in line, more like," Bet answered. "They'll wonder where he is, but we oughta have at least a week before anyone comes looking for him, and I doubt that search party'll be too intense. They won't want him back too fast. The real question we ought to be asking is, why was he coming after *us*?"

At this, Genevieve returned from behind the supply wagon, where she and Trace had been washing their clothes in a basin of horse water. Wherever they had hidden themselves away during the fight, they'd wound up covered in thick, stinking mud, and Bet had told them that they'd be walking a mile behind everyone if they didn't wash.

Now, Genevieve was as clean as she was naked, which is to say mostly. She stood, wringing out her dress with quick, impatient motions, her hair dripping across her face. "Were they coming for us? Or did y'all just run into them on the way to town?"

"They were coming this way," Leda said. "I think so, anyhow. No real way to tell, maybe we just caught 'em on a wild tear and they decided to chase us down."

"Like a dog spotting a rabbit." Amity shoved the dead sheriff with her boot again. "You sure they were on our trail?" she asked. She looked up, catching Esther's eye. "Hey, you alright there? Not about to air your paunch, are you?"

Esther shook her head. "M'alright," she muttered, and it was almost true. She didn't feel sick. She just felt far-off. The corpse looked wrong, somehow, hollow, and she couldn't make herself look away.

"This your first dead body? Or just the first time you were the one puttin' a man to bed?"

"I didn't— He's not my first," she said. She didn't bother to clarify what she'd meant, that he wasn't her first dead body. And she didn't bother to correct Amity, either, that she hadn't been the one to kill the sheriff. Because, in a way, she had.

She knew it wasn't the same. She knew that whatever she felt about him, it didn't halfway meet what Bet had a right to feel about him. And either way, she didn't want to talk to Amity about it.

"What's his name again, Leda?" Bet asked, ignoring the way the air between Esther and Amity was growing dense with challenge.

"Holthauer," Leda said without hesitation. "He's the biggest toad in the puddle between Phoenix and Flagstaff. The further we get up towards Zion, the easier it'll be to make like we don't know what happened to him, but we're too close to his den right now for me to sleep easy at night."

"That settles it," Bet said with an air of finality. "We're making tracks. Once Trace is done washing up, you two haul this bull out to the scrub and ditch him. If we're lucky, he'll get handled by the buzzards before anyone comes looking at him too close."

This last directive was pointed at Esther and Cye. Cye rolled their shoulders and sighed—not ostentatiously but enough that Esther could see how exhausted they were. She was exhausted too, in her bones and in her soul, and the thought of heaving that corpse out into the desert added weight to her shoulders. The thought of then having to walk back alone with Cye, with their long pauses and significant glances, with their dimples and their wide, watchful eyes and their graceful neck . . . it was almost too much to bear.

"Mind if I bump in?" Amity said, interrupting Esther's thoughts. "Me and Esther, we can take him on a ride. I wouldn't know the half of what needs to be done to pack up the camp," she added, glancing at Cye. "But I'd bet your right hand over there would."

Bet stared at Amity for a moment, then nodded. "You two be back here before an hour's gone, or you'll be following our tracks. Understand?"

Amity nodded, and before Esther could bother having an opinion about a change of plans, everyone but the three of them was off and working.

"Feet or head?" Amity said, pointing to the dead man that lay still on Esther's bedroll.

Esther looked at the dead man's boots. They were dirt-crusted, the toes pointing away from each other. She decided not to look at his head, which was a mess of blood and sweat, all caked in dust. There was a smell coming off the man, like baking leather and sour sweat, like piss and rage, like the burlap they reused for everyone who walked to the noose back in Valor. "I'll take the feet," she said.

"I hoped you would," Amity replied. "I hate taking the feet." She scooped her arms under Holthauer's shoulders, hooking her elbows under his armpits. His head lolled against her shirt, smearing it with streaks of dark brown. "Get along, now," Amity grunted. "We've only got an hour, and all."

Esther grabbed his feet and stood. The dead sheriff swayed between the two of them like a hammock. Carrying him away from the camp was awkward, because neither woman wanted to walk backward—there were too many pits in the earth and patches of scrub to trip over or turn an ankle on. They made slow progress away from the camp, back toward the place where all the other bandits still lay.

"I'm sorry this happened to you today," Amity said. "I'm sorry that you had to get tangled up in it."

"It's what I signed up for." Esther was breathless already from hauling the sheriff's deadweight. "I knew the risks when I joined the Librarians."

"Naw, you didn't," Amity replied easily. "You had no idea. Maybe you knew there would be adventure, and maybe you knew about how it's not always the safest proposition, being out between cities. But you didn't know death would come so close by you, and so soon. You didn't know how heavy a man gets when there's no life left in him. You don't deserve to have to know what it's like."

"Sure I do." Esther hadn't expected the words to slip out of her, but they did, easier than a coinpurse falling out of a drunk's pocket. "This is the kind of life there is for me."

They passed the fallen body of a bandit—or, Esther supposed, a deputy. His horse was long gone, vanished into the desert. The other four of his kindred lay not far off, a couple of them already attracting buzzards. Once they'd gotten twenty paces past the fallen man, Amity stopped walking.

"Here, this'll do. Don't want to spread 'em out too far from each other," she said, and she dropped Holthauer's shoulders. The weight of him jerked his ankles out of Esther's hands, and he fell to the ground like a sack of pamphlets. "What's that supposed to mean, then? The kind of life there is for you?"

Esther braced her hands on her thighs, trying to catch her breath. The sun was steadily climbing, and it was high and hot enough now to cook the sweat right out of her. "Never mind," she panted. "Do we need to do anything else to him before we get back to camp?"

"Sure do," Amity replied, pulling a broad hunting knife from a sheath Esther hadn't noticed earlier and couldn't seem to spot now. "Get his boots off. Someone'll recognize those boots if we leave 'em here."

Esther began the work of tugging the dead sheriff's boots off, which was no easy task. His leg twisted loosely in her hands, and his knee gave a baritone *pop* when she tugged hard on his ankle to dislodge his boot. "Oh," she said, the sound leaving her without her permission.

"That'll happen," Amity said. "He's not holding any muscles tense, so his joints aren't as hard to dislocate. Don't worry about being gentle, though, not like he's going to be mad at you if his feet wind up facing the wrong way." She chuckled to herself at that, then drove her knife into Holthauer's belly, burying the blade in him to the hilt. With a jerk of her wrist, she dragged the knife up toward his sternum, pausing a few times to adjust her grip as she went.

Esther managed not to scream, but it was a close call. "What are you— *Stop that!*" she shouted frantically, wanting only for Amity to stop sawing her way through the dead man's abdomen.

She got her wish. Amity paused, her knife still sheathed in Holthauer's gut, and looked at Esther with a puzzled expression. "Why?"

"Why? Well—well, why are you doing it in the first place?"

"The smell," Amity said with an easy smile. She had dimples just like Cye did, but that smile was anything but warm. "The smell will carry, and it'll call over more buzzards. Them and bugs. This way, he'll be et up before sundown. Are you done with those boots yet?"

Esther swallowed hard, returning her attention to the boot that Holthauer still wore. She yanked on it hard, wanting to be finished with this job. Wanting to be back at the camp instead of alone in the desert with Amity and that cold smile.

Amity sat back on her heels, stabbing the knife into the dirt beside her, and dug her hands into the sheriff's belly. She pulled it open with a tearing sound Esther wouldn't soon forget. Stink rose up out of him, thick as fresh stew, and Esther pulled her shirt up over her nose and mouth to try to escape the choking smell of a man's innards. "So, you think this is the only kind of life you get, is that right? Weren't figuring on Cye, I'd wager."

"I don't want to talk about this," Esther protested, her chin tucked low to try to keep her face covered by the cloth of her shirt—but then she couldn't help herself, and she let her face pop free of its refuge. "What about Cye?"

Amity laughed, a real laugh. She finished spreading Holthauer's gut and stood, holding her hands out to her sides so they wouldn't touch her clothes. "What about Cye, indeed. It's plain as the bullet in that man's skull, girl. You're sparking for them. Guessing you never felt that kind of way back home, is that right?"

"No, that's not right," Esther muttered. She gave the sheriff's boot a final tug, and it popped off his foot, knocking her back into the dust.

Amity sat down just a few feet away, rubbing her bloody hands in the dirt to clean them. "No? Well, doesn't the plot just . . . turn to mud." She laughed again, scrubbing her palms together so bloody earth fell from between them. "We've still got a little time, you know. To talk things through. Or I could teach you how to take a punch. Either one."

Esther shook her head. "It's just—I don't want to talk about this with you," she said.

"Who else are you going to talk about it with?" Amity replied, and Esther couldn't help but laugh because it was true—she couldn't tell any of the Librarians about anything, not if she wanted their respect.

"I don't want to feel any kind of way about Cye," she admitted. "I don't want to feel any kind of way about anybody. I've been down that road, and I know what's at the end of it."

"Awful worldly for a colt," Amity drawled. "What's at the end of that road, then, world traveler?"

"Nothing but trouble," Esther said. "I thought I put all that mess behind me when I left home, but I guess it followed me. I should have known better than to try to have something good." She jerked her head to one side so Amity wouldn't see her eyes filling with tears. She blinked furiously, trying not to cry. "I should have known better."

"So, that's it, then," Amity said. She picked up a fresh fistful of desert sand and rubbed it across her wrists, scouring away more blood with every pass of her quick, clever hands. "You think you don't get anything good, because you feel the wrong way about the wrong people."

Blinking couldn't hold the tears back anymore, not now that Amity'd said it out loud. "I do," Esther said, unable to keep the hitch out of her voice. "I feel the wrong way about the wrong people and I know what kind of life there is for me, and I thought I could outrun it but I *can't*." Esther felt the heavy weight of Amity's arm across her shoulders, and before she knew what she was doing, she told the whole tale.

Her and Beatriz, and what they'd been to each other, and the feelings they'd fought until the fight was lost. A whole secret year together, that's what they'd gotten, and they'd both known the whole time that it couldn't end but in tragedy. "That's what happens to people like us," Esther gasped, her voice thick with tears. "We go wrong and then we get our comeuppance. And Beatriz—"

"Beatriz got her comeuppance?" Amity finished, giving Esther's shoulders a squeeze. Esther nodded, hiccupping. "What was it? Did her daddy beat her?"

Esther shook her head, and the thick haze that came with crying seemed to clear away all at once, replaced by something cold and cutting. "No," she said. "My daddy hanged her." Amity drew in a sharp breath, and Esther felt a strange sense of satisfaction: *yes, it really was that bad.* "Someone reported her for Unapproved Materials, and she hanged right in front of me. So, you see? We went wrong, and she paid for it. I know my bill's in the mail," she added bitterly. "Just a matter of time before I get what's coming to me. But I thought that maybe—

maybe if I did enough good, if I just stayed on the right path and stuck with the Librarians and didn't lay eyes on another girl the way I laid eyes on Beatriz . . . maybe I'd be alright. Maybe I wouldn't bring hurt to anyone else's life." She wiped her face off on her sleeves, smearing grime across her cheeks in the process. "I guess that was stupid."

Amity leaned back onto her elbows and sighed. "Yeah," she said. "Most of what you say is stupid, though, so I wouldn't read too much into it."

Esther let out a startled laugh. "Now, wait just a minute," she said, but she didn't have anything to follow it up with, so she laughed again.

"You really believe all that? About how there's only one end in sight for people like you?" Amity said, tipping her chin back toward the sky and pulling her hat partway down her face, so only her nose and mouth were visible. "Horseshit. You only think that because you've never seen different." Esther started to reply, but Amity held up a still-bloody finger. "Don't interrupt me, pup. You know I'm right. You're a woman and you love people who aren't men, is that right?"

Esther hesitated to make sure she wasn't interrupting. "That's right," she said, "but—"

"No *but,* it's just true," Amity said, proving that her rule about interruptions only ran in one direction. "And you've only ever read stories about people like you, right? You've never met one of your kind before now. Well, except for Beatriz," she added. "Ain't that so?"

"Yeah," Esther answered reluctantly. She sensed a trap coming, but she couldn't figure out how to step around it.

"All those stories you've read," Amity said softly, pulling her hat back off her eyes by a few degrees. "Who gave 'em to you?"

"The Librarians," Esther said.

"And who gave 'em to the Librarians?"

Esther thought hard about that one. The things the Librarians brought weren't subject to the Textbook Approval and Research Council, since they only worked on schoolbooks, and they weren't subject to the Media Review Committee, since they mostly did film and television. "The Board of Materials Approval?" she guessed.

Amity nodded. "And what do you think that Board wants you to believe about yourself?" She paused, but it wasn't the kind of pause that wants an answer. "You might not have a happy ending coming to you, Hopalong. But if you come to a bad end, it won't be on account of what kind of person you fall for. I've seen a lot more of the world than you have, and I can tell you upright: I've seen as many good ends as bad ones for your kind of heart."

With that, Amity stood, brushing dried blood and desert sand from her hands. She rose to her full height like a snake uncoiling, graceful and smooth and sudden all at once. Just the way she'd mounted her horse the first time Esther saw her—like quicksilver, in one place and then in the next as if there was no world in her way. She loped back over to the sheriff's body, bent down, and plucked the silver star from the inside face of his lapel. "Hid this thing away so we couldn't see it," she muttered, "but couldn't stand to take it all the way off." She buffed the blood off it until she could see the eagle stamped into the silver, then tucked it into her pocket. "That's our time spent," she said, offering a grimy hand to help Esther stand up. After a moment's hesitation, Esther took it. "Don't leave those boots, bring 'em with us," Amity said.

Esther did as she was told, carrying one boot in each hand. The sun climbed a little higher in the sky, beating the sweat out of the two women as they made their way back to the camp. Esther wiped her forehead with the back of her wrist, pointed her feet toward the wagons in the far distance—toward Cye. As they walked, something occurred to her.

"You said before, about teaching me how to take a punch," she said.

"So I did," Amity replied.

"Is that offer still good?" Esther asked. "Only . . . I'd like to sort out how to punch, and how to shoot. Just in case something else bad comes around."

Amity nodded. "Sure thing, Hopalong," she said. "I'll give you lessons. But only if you make me a promise."

"What kind of a promise?" Esther asked.

"You've got to stop waiting to be told you're allowed to do things," Amity said. She didn't look at her, kept loping along as casual as a fed coyote. "You've got to promise me you'll stop being too scared to piss without permission."

"I don't—" Esther started to protest, but then she remembered that she *had* asked Bet's permission to stop riding the day before, and she swallowed the rest of her sentence. "Okay," she said. "I promise."

They lapsed into the kind of companionable silence that follows tears, and as they picked their way through the scrub, Esther wondered if Amity was right. Maybe, she thought, just *maybe* it was possible.

Between Esther and the horizon, the wagons shimmered in the heat. She knew that they weren't an oasis— no cool shade or sweet water was waiting for her there. But they weren't a mirage, either, and that hope felt like just enough to fit in her fists.

CHAPTER

6

The moment Esther and Amity returned to the wagons, Cye was in Esther's ear like a cactus owl in the hollow of a saguaro. "Here, this should be the last of it," they said, thrusting a huge, precarious bundle of blankets and cooking pots into her arms. "Sort these into the supply wagon. And don't go losing yourself in those blankets again, hear?"

"Sure," Esther muttered. "Taking the corpse out into the desert was fine, thanks for asking."

"What was that?" Cye called over their shoulder as they jogged toward the horses—but they didn't wait to hear an answer.

Amity clapped Esther on the shoulder with one strong hand. "Good luck with that," she said, her tone not revealing whether she meant the supplies or the infuriating Apprentice Librarian.

"Do you want to sort it out with me?" Esther asked hopefully.

"Oh, I wish I could, but I'm afraid I've got something

urgent to attend to," Amity replied. She ambled over to a pile of bedrolls that were waiting to be strapped to the horses and sat down with her back against them. She tilted her hat over her head again, just as she had in the desert, and folded her hands across her belly. Esther watched, indignant. After a minute, Amity reached into her shirt pocket and pulled out a toothpick, settling it between her front teeth to worry at.

Esther shook her head, turning toward the supply wagon. "That's just *fine*," she grumbled into the unstable bundle again, trying to make her way across the gravel and sand without tripping over anything.

She didn't mean to move quietly, but her steps were so slow and so careful that Bet and Leda didn't hear her approach. She didn't mean to sneak up on them, but they were so involved in their conversation that they didn't seem to notice her at all, and she was so focused on trying not to drop anything that she didn't notice them, either.

Not until she'd deposited her armful of detritus in the back of the wagon.

She climbed into the wagon and started trying to figure out where the cooking pots were supposed to go—she knew that they had specific homes, and Leda was especially particular about the way they were arranged. As she stared at two similar pots, trying to determine which was meant to go where, Bet and Leda's voices drifted in to her.

She didn't mean to eavesdrop. Not until she heard her own name.

". . . Esther is trustworthy." That was Bet, and she didn't sound happy. Esther wondered what the beginning of that sentence had been.

"Why would it be her?" Leda replied. Both of them were speaking softly, in tones that weren't intended to carry. Esther held her breath—if they caught her listening in, they'd think she was spying. They would send her out into the desert to die, maybe putting a bullet in her back to make sure she wouldn't tell anyone their secrets.

"I can't think of any other reason the sheriff would come after us," Bet hissed. "She must have told someone something. Or, at best, someone saw her and sent word to the authorities that we kidnapped her. A girl like her, with a father like the one she's got? Sure, they'd shoot at us to get her home."

Leda's sigh was almost too soft to hear, but Esther was listening so hard that she caught the edge of it. "Even if you're right," Leda said, "there's nothing we can do. We can't send her home."

"We could shoot her," Bet replied, her voice suddenly cold. "Leave her with the bandits in the desert."

"On a hunch?" Leda snapped. Bet shushed her, and

her voice dropped again. "Lisbeth. If you need me to tell you not to make that kind of a mess, I will. But you and I both know you're not about to shoot that girl, not after what she told us about what she's running from."

There was a long silence. Esther's legs were beginning to cramp and tremble, and she wasn't sure how long she'd be able to hold up the cooking pot that was in her arms—it seemed to get heavier with every word that Bet and Leda dropped into it.

Finally, after what felt like far too long—"You're right. Damn it," Bet muttered. Esther could hear shuffling, followed by the soft sound of a kiss. "I just don't understand it," Bet said again. In the absence of that cold, hard edge, her voice just sounded tired. "I don't know why he would come after us. We're employees of the State. There's no reason for any authorities to mess us around."

"They'll do what they do," Leda replied. "Meantime, we just need to get that girl to Utah. We'll drop her there, and she won't be our problem anymore. She won't be a danger to us, nor a burden. Ten days, Bet. Ten days at the most. We've gotten through worse than that. Hell, remember Odessa?"

Bet laughed at this, and Leda laughed too. There was the sound of another kiss, longer this time, followed by fading footsteps crunching through the gravel. Their voices continued, but as they walked away from the supply wagon, they became too soft for Esther to follow.

She let herself breathe again, dropping the cookpot next to its fellows without concerning herself with order.

A threat. That's what she was to them. Or, at best, a *burden.*

They didn't see her as part of the team at all. They saw her as something to be got rid of, a stray dog that wouldn't stop following them unless they threw it scraps. A magnet for disaster.

A magnet for tragedy.

Even though she could afford to breathe as loud as she wanted, Esther suddenly felt like she couldn't get a lungful of air for all the ration tickets in Austin. Just when she'd started to think that maybe things could be different—just when Amity had convinced her that maybe she could write her own end—she had to go and overhear Bet and Leda. They clearly thought she was responsible for the deaths of those bandits, the lather on the horses, the gunpowder spent in the desert that morning.

She could see it right there before her, easy to grab as a saddle horn: despair. She could give up then and there.

Part of her thought it would be simpler that way, easier. Part of her thought it was inevitable.

But part of her, the part that had come alive in the

desert as she cried all over Amity—part of her could see another way. Bet and Leda might think she was a curse, might think she was deadweight. But she didn't have to let them keep on thinking it.

She could change their mind.

She could write her own end. She could do it without asking anyone's permission, just like Amity'd said. She knew it. She clenched her fists, resolved. She had run away from home, and she had convinced Bet to let her stay on, and she had ridden a horse for two straight days, and she had fought with bandits—with a posse—and she had *won*. She had dragged a body to the desert and watched over her shoulder as buzzards circled over it.

She had done all of that, all things she would have thought impossible just a week before.

If she could do all of those things, she could do this, too.

She belonged with the Librarians, and she would prove it.

✎

That day's ride was the hardest one yet. Esther was saddlesore from riding during the fight with the bandits, and her back and arms trembled from the exertion of carrying Holthauer into the desert, and her heart ached with the knowledge that Bet and Leda wanted her gone. She followed the wagons, wincing with the ceaseless motion of the horse beneath her. That evening, as the group set up camp just a few miles outside the city of Endurance, Esther remained quiet, thinking.

It was easy enough to maintain her silence: there was to be no campfire that night, no bright signal to summon anyone who would be looking after the sheriff and his posse. They chewed uncooked rations in exhausted silence—hard bread unsoftened by stew, too-salty meat that left Esther's mouth raw and dry. After they ate, Amity was gripped by a strange burst of energy, and she insisted on teaching Esther how to throw a punch and how to dodge one. She tried to get into shooting, too, getting as far as showing Esther how to cock the hammer of a revolver before Bet threatened to give a shooting demonstration herself if they didn't quiet down.

They went their separate ways for the evening, bundling themselves into their bedrolls before the chill of the desert evening could sap the warmth from them entirely. The sleep that overtook Esther was deep, almost violently so, and dreamless.

She woke before the last stars had winked out of the sky, and when she did, she had a plan.

CHAPTER

7

Endurance was easy to find, once Esther got her horse to the main road. She just had to follow the flags.

The highways had fallen into serious disrepair some time before, just like any other street. Esther knew that they'd been smooth as glass once, before the money to keep them that way got soaked up by the money-sponge that was War. Nowadays, the best roads were paved with pea gravel—smooth enough not to hurt a horse's hooves, if it was unshod, and easy to rake even.

The worst ones, of course, were pocked with pot-holes, uneven and puddled. Those were horsebreak roads, roads where a patch of water might be an inch deep or a foot, roads that ruined ankles. Those roads needed to be busted up, but doing the work by hand was ruinously difficult, and doing the work with machines meant allocating diesel for the job. A pea-gravel high-way was the sign of a very wealthy town, indeed—a town that had managed to stretch a road-breaking crew all the way outside of city limits, that kept the road raked and even, was a town that had either Defense money or a whole stash of diesel to use.

The roads in Valor had been a mixed bunch, always in progress, always the subject of fundraisers and hasty repairs and town-hall meetings. The road to Endurance, on the other hand, stretched ahead of Esther like a river of gray, very nearly gleaming in the thin light of the lightening sky. The road was straight, flanked on either side by a wide expanse of desert. Esther shivered atop her horse, listening to the nighttime sounds of the things that lived there in this unlivable place, and kept her eyes locked on the two bright flags that fluttered in the distance.

They were enormous. They were signal flags, flags to indicate that there was a city here and that the city was loyal to the State. Flags that would be visible from high up in the air, just in case someone flying overhead wasn't sure whether Endurance was a haven or a target. Flags that everyone in the city would be able to see by sunlight during the day, by spotlight at night. Valor had the same flags, although they weren't so large, and Esther's city couldn't afford the electricity to keep them lit up every night—just on holidays. They dominated the horizon. They would be, Esther knew, replicated in miniature throughout the city, in school classrooms and front porches and windows. Esther's father had always said that the flags were supposed to be a reminder of what the citizens were fighting for, what they were sacrificing for. They were a reminder of what was most important: the State, and the War, and everyone working together to keep both of those things going strong.

It struck Esther, suddenly, that the Librarians didn't seem to have a flag. There wasn't one painted on either wagon, wasn't one draped across the canvas of the wagon cover. She hadn't recalled seeing one folded up in the supply wagon, either.

She made a mental note to raise the issue with Bet and Leda. Surely, it was dangerous to them, she thought, not having a flag. Surely, someone would ask why they didn't have one, someday in town.

As she rode her horse toward those two massive flags, Esther tried hard not to chew on her loyalties and where they might lie. She was sure that she wanted to be a Librarian, that she wanted to find a life where she could be something other than a curse. And she was sure that the Librarians weren't friends of the State—they couldn't be, not the way they lived. Not the way they talked.

Esther shifted in the saddle, her soreness from the punching lesson of the night before stacking on top of the ache that came with days of riding. She watched the flags grow larger, and she tried not to ask herself what that meant about her. What it meant about who her enemies might be and who she might have to hate.

What it meant about who might already hate her.

"I'm not going to think about that right now," she muttered aloud, hoping that hearing the words would make them true. Her horse's ears twitched at the sound of her voice, and she tried again. "I'm not going to think about it," she told it. She touched her shirt pocket with light fingers, feeling the crinkle of Cye's stolen identity papers alongside the supply list she'd scribbled down by moonlight. "I'm going to get to town, and I'm going to get supplies and bring them back, and that'll be all." The horse snorted the exact same way it had throughout their ride, but Esther replied as though the sound was a unique one. "It'll work," she said without conviction. "And if it doesn't, at least I'll have fresh rags to sit on tomorrow. It's not like they can hate me more."

This time, the horse did not reply, and they spent the remainder of the ride in silence.

By the time they passed between those two enormous flags, dawn was creeping over the mountains that marked the horizon. The Librarians would be awake by now, Esther knew—she only had to hope that they would find the note she'd pinned to her bedroll, and that they would wait for her to return before packing up their camp and leaving for the day.

If they didn't wait for her, she reminded herself, she would just be on the road without a plan. Again.

She'd done it before. It wasn't so scary now as it had been then.

The flags flapped overhead, but they were high enough above Esther that she couldn't hear them snapping, nor could she feel the wind that stirred them. Nevertheless, her horse shifted uneasily at the movement of the fabric and the sound of the halyard snapping against the flagpole.

"You'll want to walk that horse in town instead of riding it," the checkpoint guard below the flags said lazily as he scanned the identity papers Esther handed him—Cye's identity papers. He spat a lipful of brown saliva into a small tin bucket on his desk, adjusted the woven blanket that rested across his shoulders to ward off the damp cold of the early morning. It was a chill that the three walls of the guardhouse didn't do a thing to stave off, Esther was sure. "People in town don't like to see a lady up top of them. Makes it hard to give her a proper *howdy*."

He smiled, and Esther smiled back, because that smile meant he wasn't going to question her identity. He wasn't looking at it closely, was paying more attention to her. "Oh, sure," she said, using the warm, quiet voice she'd always relied on to keep men happy. It was a tone that said she wasn't a threat, wasn't going to laugh at them, was maybe a little impressed by them for a reason she wouldn't reveal. "Would you be willing to give me a hand down? I'm just about stuck up here, froze onto this darn saddle." She gave a little shiver, and the checkpoint guard's smile warmed just as she'd known it would.

"What's his name?" the guard asked, easing his way over to her and bracing a hand on the horse's shoulder.

Esther had no idea. She hadn't retained the names of any of the horses, in spite of Cye's best efforts to impress them upon her. She tried to think of one, a lie, and the only thing that came into her head was awful, but she didn't figure as she had a choice, so she said it.

"Silas." She forced her smile a notch brighter. "His name's Silas."

She'd never wanted to think of Silas Whitmour again, not after the last time she'd seen him. Not after the way he'd stared at her while Beatriz snapped at the end of a rope. He'd looked at her like she was something to own and use and break, and now, here she was, as far away from him as she could muster, using his name on a horse that deserved better.

"That's a fine name for a horse," the guard said agreeably, his eyes on Esther's collarbone.

She let her hand linger on his shoulder for a moment as she dismounted, and she hated herself for it, for all of it. For charming him. She hated herself, because she didn't rightly know why she was bothering to do it—she didn't need anything from him other than safe and free passage in and out of Endurance. But she did it anyway, more of a compulsion than a reflex. Her speech drifted to the familiar, the ungrammatical, the helpless. She caught herself tucking her chin down, trying to make herself look just a little shy.

The guard handed her a daylong pass, one that marked her not as a citizen of Endurance but as a known quantity who could stay until sundown. He winked at her, and she was flooded again with that hateful relief: This man liked her. This man would be nice to her. This man hadn't guessed any of her secrets. "Go on, then, and get what you need before the heat gets to suffering. You and Silas here'll want to be back at wherever you're camped before then." Esther tucked the day pass into her shirt pocket alongside the rest of her stolen papers and thanked the guard—but before she could get more than a few steps away from him, he called out to her again. "Oh, hold a minute. Get back here, now."

Esther's gut clenched in a spasm of terror. She hadn't planned for this part—she hadn't planned for what would happen if she didn't get through the checkpoint. Why hadn't she planned for this? She was stricken by her own naivete, that she might think she could just wander into Endurance, blithe as a lizard sunning itself on the frame of a gallows.

She swallowed hard, her throat tight with fear, and turned to face the guard.

"I almost forgot," he said, extending a hand toward her. The hand held a piece of paper, thin as newsprint, the size of a playing card. "I'm s'posed to hand these to anyone who's leaving town, but you might want it now. If you've seen her on your travels, you stop at the police station and let them know right away. They're right in the middle of town, in the Patriot Square Pavilion." He grinned, his lower lip bulging with chaw. "You couldn't miss it if you was a drunk mule with a blindfold on."

Esther took the paper he was holding out to her, marveling at the steadiness of her hand. She pretended to look at it, then folded it in half and tucked it into her shirt pocket. "Thank you so much," she said, her tongue thick and half-numb with a combination of relief and draining panic. "I'm sure I'll see you again on my way out."

"I'm sure you will," he said, tipping his hat. With that, the guard stepped back behind his desk in the little open-walled guardhouse. Esther walked away, waiting to hear him calling out to her again, but he didn't. Still, she couldn't breathe quite right again until she was a few minutes' walk into Endurance, when she was sure he wouldn't come chasing after her.

The streets were empty—it was too early for anyone

but the milkman to be out—but she couldn't afford to look suspicious, just in case that milkman came walking by. She tied her horse to the first hitching post she found and braced her hands against the saddle, pretending to adjust a stirrup until she could stop shaking. "Okay," she whispered. "Okay. It's alright. You did it. Just get the supplies and get out. This was the whole point."

The horse didn't respond.

Esther reached into her shirt pocket to pull out the list of supplies, figuring she'd start at the grocery and then work her way around Endurance to get the bits and pieces she couldn't find there. She grabbed Cye's identity papers by mistake. She tucked them away again, not knowing whether they'd be checked at the various stores she needed to visit, and reached back into the pocket.

She didn't come away with the list that time, either. Her fingers found that newsprint-thin paper instead. She didn't remember putting it into her shirt pocket, didn't even remember taking it from the guard—she only remembered watching his face for any sign that he was about to draw his revolver and finish their conversation with talking-iron.

She unfolded it now, with fingers that wouldn't stop shaking even though the danger had passed. What he'd handed her, she found, was a miniature version of the wanted posters that hung in every grocery store, post office, and town hall. *WANTED Dead or Alive,* it began in tall, bold letters—and then beneath those, a description of the crime. *For the murder by Assassination of Mason Turlock, Vice-President of the Southwest Territory. Any information about this individual to be reported to authorities immediately. Unlawful withholding of information about wanted individuals is a State and Federal Crime,* it continued.

Esther's breath caught in her throat. She hadn't heard about the assassination. Hell, she'd been away from cities for long enough that she hadn't so much as seen a flag at half-mast the day it happened. But her surprise at the news wasn't what made her breath catch.

It was the sketch below the description of the crime. That was what stuck Esther, hard as a cactus quill.

The sketch looked familiar, and the name below it, printed in the same tall, bold letters as the word *WANTED*—that name looked familiar, too.

BUSTER "AMITY" COLE, INSURRECTIONIST ASSASSIN

Esther stared at the sketch and the name for a long time, but being ink on paper, none of it changed. There could be no question about what she was seeing.

The woman on the page was Amity, and it seemed that she was going to be a sight more trouble than she'd let on.

The sun was high and cruel when Esther returned to the camp, and the heat was precisely as oppressive as the guard at Endurance had warned it would be. She wasn't sweating nearly enough: the dry, wavering press of the open desert had pulled the sweat out of her and tossed it away like spat tobacco. She knew this wasn't good—a person couldn't rightly grow up in Valor without learning to recognize the signs of heatstroke—but she couldn't pull water out of thin air, so she just kept riding until she spotted the shimmering shade of the wagons.

She didn't so much dismount her horse as fall sideways off it. The horse dipped its nose into the wagon-shaded bucket of water that the horses all shared, but it didn't gulp the water down the way Esther would have. It had done a smarter job drinking water in town than she had, drinking every time she tied it up at a hitching post.

She'd managed to get hold of all the supplies on the

Librarians' list—food and fresh rags and socks and snuff, bullets and thread and grease, everything they'd run out of and everything they'd need for the next leg of the journey. But she hadn't thought to drink a single sip of water that whole time. Her mind had been fixed hard to the wanted poster with Amity's face on it. She could hardly remember a single interaction she'd had with a shopkeeper; she'd spent the entire time trying to decide what to do with the information in her shirt pocket.

"Where the fuck have you been, Hopalong?" Cye stomped around the side of the wagon, their eyes as hard and sparking as a flintlock. "Aw, hell," they said, looking at her face. "You look like you've got a buzzard following you, and for cause. Sit down before you fall down." They pointed at the ground next to the wagon wheel, and Esther wanted to argue, but her knees acquiesced for her, and before she knew how she got on the ground, her back was resting against the wide, flat spokes of the wheel.

"I went to town," she rasped hoarsely, lifting her chin to her horse's saddlebags.

"How did you get through the checkpoint?" Cye asked, whipping off their kerchief and dunking it in the bucket of horse-water. They lifted it over Esther's head, and before she could protest, they wrung it out.

The water that fell over her may have been tainted

with horse drool, but it felt like heaven anyway. She closed her eyes as it dripped across her face, felt it evaporate into the too-close air before it could reach her chest. "I stole your papers," she whispered, smiling at the indignant noise that came out of Cye. "Here," she said, and she reached into her shirt pocket. She handed the papers over with her eyes still closed. "You wouldn't want those getting dripped on."

Cye wrung out another kerchief of horse-water over Esther's head, then handed her the damp cloth. "Press that over your throat," they said. "Cool yourself a few degrees. I'll get water."

Their footsteps passed in front of her and faded around the corner, and Esther pressed the cloth to the sides of her neck, sighing at the cool relief of it. There was nothing but her and that cool cloth for the next thirty seconds—nothing but the feeling of heat leaching out of her body at last.

At the end of that blissful thirty seconds, Cye's footsteps returned, and Esther felt the slight *thump* as their weight landed on the ground beside her.

"Drink," they said, and Esther cracked one eye to see them holding out a canteen. "Just a little at a time," they added. Esther tried to take a small sip, but once the water touched her tongue, she found herself gulping at the water desperately. It was sweet, it was cool, she needed it— "Whoa, there," Cye said, their cool fingers folding over her hot, swollen ones. They eased the canteen away from her mouth.

"No," Esther mewled softly, the sound coming out of her involuntarily.

"You need to slow down, or you'll make yourself sick and lose it all up again," Cye said. "Sorry, Hopalong."

"Right," she said. "You're right, I'm sorry. I couldn't help it."

"I know," they murmured. Their hands were still over hers, the pad of their thumbs resting over the knuckles of her own. Esther could feel her pulse in her palms, and she wondered if Cye could feel it too, could feel how fast it was coming. "It's alright. What the hell were you thinking?"

She shook her head. "I wanted—I wanted to prove I'm useful."

"Ain't useful if you're dead." They gave her a small, rare smile. "Damn foolish, riding into the desert on your own."

She nodded and returned the smile, her eyes sinking into that impossible dimple. "I'm damn foolish, I suppose," she said. "Are Bet and Leda angry?"

"They don't know you were gone, but they were about to get their backs up at you for sleeping in," Cye said. "Drink a little more before you go talk to them. You can't make your case if you faint at 'em."

Esther drank a little more, less desperately this time. As she did, she wondered if she should tell Cye what she learned in Endurance, or if she should save it for Bet and Leda. She knew she had to tell them—she had to prove her loyalty, had to make sure they knew that she wasn't the one who had drawn the sheriff their way. And if they didn't know who Amity was—well. Whether they hated her or not, she couldn't let them keep riding around with a murderer unawares.

She touched her hand to her shirt pocket, and her heart sank.

"Cye," she said tentatively. "I don't suppose I could see your papers back again, could I?"

Cye touched the back of their hand to her forehead. "Funny," they said. "Your skin don't feel so clammy as it did before. Seems you're recovering from the heat, but you're still talking like your brain's been baked. Why in the hell would I give a thief back my silver?"

Esther grimaced. "I'm sorry," she said, but Cye shook their head, grinning.

"I'm not mad you took it," they said. "Hell, if you could get into my saddlebag and pull my papers out without me hearing, you deserved what you took. But I ain't handing them right to you."

"I . . ." Esther picked up Cye's kerchief from where it had dropped into her lap, wringing it in her hands. It was already bone-dry. "I left something of mine mixed up in there. I need it back so I can talk to Bet and Leda about it," she said.

Cye raised an eyebrow, nakedly curious and not about to go unsatisfied. "Now, is that right?" they drawled. "Well, let's just see if I can find it out for you." Esther swore to herself as Cye drew their identity papers from their own shirt pocket with a flourish. They began to flip through the papers. "Is it your grocery list?" They held up the supply list with a smile that said they were going to draw this out for just as long as they could. "Your handwriting is appalling, Hopalong."

"I wrote it with no light," Esther said miserably. "Please, Cye—"

"No, I think maybe it's not this." Cye crumpled up the list and tucked it into Esther's still-unbuttoned pocket with care. They were close enough to breathe in, all clean sweat and fresh pomade. It occurred to Esther that they could have simply handed the list back to her— but before she could dwell on it, the brief warmth of their fingers was gone. "Let's see what else might be in here." They continued flipping through their papers until they found the tiny folded wanted poster, nested between the authorization to travel between territories and the authorization to purchase bullets. "What might this be?"

"Please, don't," Esther said, but it was too late. Cye

had already unfolded the paper. In a matter of seconds, the mischief in their face faded, replaced by a guarded, wary confusion.

"What's this about?" they asked. "Is this—is this some kind of a joke?"

"I don't think it's a joke," Esther said. "I think it's damned serious."

"But this looks like Amity," Cye said. When they looked up at Esther, their eyes were pleading for any explanation other than the obvious one.

Esther chewed on her lip. "Yeah, and her name looks like Amity's too, don't it?"

"Doesn't," Cye muttered vaguely, an obvious reflex. "Librarians gotta talk straight. Don't get bad habits, Hopalong."

Before Esther could reply, a pair of shadows came around the corner of the wagon. The shadows were attached at the feet to Bet and Leda.

"There you are," Bet snapped. "Where in the festering hell have you been? We need to get gaited, and we need to do it yesterday."

Cye and Esther looked up at Bet and Leda, neither of them able to conceal their anguish.

"Stowaway's got some news from the city," Cye said, their voice hoarse with dread. "I reckon you three ought to find a patch of quiet."

"What's this about?" Bet asked, impatient. "Here's plenty quiet. Get to talkin'."

Cye scrambled to their feet, holding their hand out to Esther to help her up. "Sorry, boss," they said. "I need to unload this horse before she sweats herself into jerky. I'll ask Amity to help me," they added, giving Esther a significant look.

"I'll thank you for it," Esther said to them, and she meant it—the supply wagon where they'd unpack the horse was on the opposite side of the camp, so there would be no risk of Amity overhearing what Esther had to tell Bet and Leda. Cye tipped their hat to her and took the horse by the reins, leading it out of the shade.

Leda's jaw worked like she was chewing at the inside of her cheek. She narrowed her eyes at Esther, her gaze merciless. "And what," she said, her words heavy with danger, "was in those saddlebags?"

Esther kept her chin steady, summoning gallows courage. It was strength enough to look right back at Leda and answer with a voice that passed for certain: "Supplies. From Endurance."

Surprise was plain on Bet's face, just as anger was plain on Leda's. It was Bet who spoke first. "You rode to Endurance? Today?"

"I did," Esther answered. The little folded paper fluttered between her fingertips. "I took Cye's papers with me, and I got everything on your list," she added, nodding to Leda. "It's all there. I paid out of my own pocket, too, so as not to steal from you." Stealing from Leda seemed like a far more dangerous proposition than riding into Endurance alone.

"Were you seen?" Bet asked urgently. "Were you followed?"

"Not so far's I can tell," Esther said. "But listen—there's something you need to—"

"Stupid as spurs on a jackrabbit," Bet snapped. "You could have gotten lost in that desert and killed a perfectly good horse on your way to nowhere. I'd bet my left boot you've led another posse back to us. Did it ever occur to you that they're looking for your damn *face*?"

"They're not," Esther snapped back. At her tone—at her daring—Bet and Leda both looked impressed, in the same way one might look impressed at a cat that's been trained to play the piano. They were silent in their surprise, only for a second, but that second was all Esther needed. "Here," she said, and she held out the miniature wanted poster, and no matter how angry Bet and Leda were, they couldn't fail to see what was in front of them.

"Aw, hell," Leda whispered. Bet sucked her teeth.

"She's an assassin," Esther said. It was the thing that was right there between them, the thing they all knew now and couldn't ignore. "She works for the insurrectionists."

Leda's lips twitched up into a grim half smile. "We prefer *resistance,*" she said.

Esther shook her head, irritated. The movement was a little too sharp, and she wasn't quite recovered from the heat yet—her vision swam and she squeezed her eyes shut for a moment before continuing. "She works for them," Esther said, "and the State is looking for her. She's the reason that sheriff came after us." She thought, but did not add: *It wasn't me. I wasn't the reason we had to kill that man.*

Bet sighed, pressing the heels of her hands into her eyes. "I reckon you're right," she said. "They're not handing out posters with anyone else's face on 'em, and Amity was riding high in front with me when we passed through the last checkpoint."

"She lied to us," Leda muttered, snatching the paper out of Esther's hand. A strange look came over her face, and her eyes cut sideways to look at Bet. "You didn't know about this, did you?"

"'Course not," Bet said, sighing. She looked at Leda, then said it again. "Leda. Of course I didn't know. I would have told you, straight out the barrel."

Leda nodded. "Thought so. But—"

"But nothing," Bet said softly. Her eyes were locked

on Leda's—Esther may as well have been a mirage in the distance, for all the notice either of them were paying her. "I don't lie to you, and secrets count for lies."

"I know it, Lisbet," Leda murmured. She bumped her forehead against Bet's briefly, a physical shorthand for some longer moment of their past, one that Esther knew must have involved trust and promises and a longer version of Bet's name that was surely forbidden to all but Leda.

It was a moment too intimate to be watched, and Esther's discomfort was almost as profound as her yearning. Something deep in her longed for a day when she would have a little signal, shared with someone who cared enough about her to stop everything in its tracks to make sure she knew she could trust them. A love like theirs—she couldn't seem to suffocate the piece of her that wanted it for herself, and somewhere in the time since Amity had let her cry in the desert, she'd stopped trying.

She couldn't quite believe that Amity was the same as the woman on the poster, but the picture was right there, and a man was dead.

And they were all in danger because of it.

Esther cleared her throat. Bet and Leda both startled, as if they'd entirely forgotten she was there, and she didn't doubt that they had.

"Right," Bet said. "Well, I suppose there's no way around it."

Leda nodded. "She can't come with us," she said. "It's too dangerous, her being recognized already. Puts the whole outfit in trouble."

Bet settled her hat over her hair, decided. "You two get the horses tacked up. I'll go find Amity and talk to her about all this, and then we can make tracks. Shouldn't take long." She shook her head. "Shame. I liked her more than any of this."

"I like you too, Bet." Amity sauntered around the corner of the supply wagon, her gait and posture too casual for the cannons in her hands. She held them low at her hips, but they were pointed at Bet and Leda, one for each. "And I like you, Leda. But—and I do hate to pick favorites," she said, sounding genuinely regretful, "I have to admit that I like Esther better than either of you."

And with that, quick as a scorpion's stinger, she struck. In a flash, one of her revolvers was holstered, and the hand that'd held it was gripping Esther by the arm.

"Sorry, Hopalong. I never wanted to use you for leverage," Amity drawled, her breath hot against Esther's shoulder. She drew Esther in close, wrapping her up in an embrace that would have been intimate if not for the gun barrel that pressed hard against Esther's side. "And say, no hard feelings for snitching on me. We're square now, I reckon." She nudged Esther with the gun. "Say it."

Bet was standing as still as a possum hit by a patroller's floodlight, but Leda nodded at Esther. "Go on, then," she said softly.

Esther swallowed hard. "We're square, Amity," she said. "Now, what'll it be?"

Amity smiled, her cheek plumping up in Esther's peripheral vision. "I thought you'd never ask."

"This don't have to go sour," Amity said easily. She rested her cheek against the top of Esther's head. "You know more about me now than you did this time yesterday. Maybe by tomorrow, you'll know what my favorite color is, too."

"It ain't yellow," Bet intoned. "No kind of coward could pull the con you just tried."

Out of the corner of her eye, Esther saw Amity give the Head Librarian an appreciative nod. "Thanks for that."

"Don't thank me yet," Bet said, folding her arms. Her posture was taut—she was ready for all of this to go wrong. Esther didn't like seeing her hands get farther away from her life preservers, but she supposed there was no way for Amity to take a bullet without it passing through Esther's own belly first.

Oh, Esther thought, clarity washing over her like cool water. *Oh. I'm a human shield.*

"You can't stay with us," Leda said, shaking her head. "I'm sorry, Amity. You must know how much we all admire the work you did to get on that poster, but you're putting us in danger. We can't get you to Utah."

"I think you can," Amity said. Her persuader was still pressed against Esther's ribs—not so painfully as it had at first, though.

Esther wondered if Amity was letting up, or settling in for a long negotiation. "Please could I sit down?" She asked it carefully, in the same soft, easy voice she had used for the officer at the checkpoint. "I'm still a little light-headed from the ride."

"You'll sit down soon enough, my girl," Amity drawled. "We won't be talking for long."

"There's nothing to discuss," Bet interrupted. "You're putting our entire operation in danger. We'll be doing damage control anyway, trying to fix any rumors that we're associated with the resistance. We won't be able to distribute Unapproved Materials for months. You've compromised our work enough as it is, Amity."

"My work's in a different weight class from yours," Amity said, a sharp edge on the words. It was a tone Esther recognized, the kind of dangerous that would have been hard to notice if she hadn't heard it a hundred times before. It was the danger of assumed authority.

Amity thought of herself as more important than the Librarians, thought her work was more urgent.

Esther had grown up in a house with that same kind of importance. She knew what happened when it was challenged. She knew what people who thought of themselves that way would do, just to protect the idea that they had the right to do it.

She didn't have a way to find out if Bet and Leda knew the same thing she did. She couldn't tell if they also heard that warning tone, that growing undercurrent of don't-try-me. Their faces betrayed nothing.

Esther was, she realized, nothing more than a hand of cards in a poker game between these three women. She was only a symbol. She wasn't the thing they were playing for. And like a bad hand, she could be discarded at any moment.

"Please," she said again, desperate to put out the fuse that was rapidly burning between the three women. "I'd really like to sit down. We can all talk about this over some water—"

"You'll want to stop talking," Amity growled in her ear, pressing the gun a little harder into Esther's side. "This doesn't really concern you."

"It hardly concerns you, either," Leda snapped. Bet's eyes cut to her, and Esther wondered if Leda was pushing too hard. "You can go to Utah if you want, Amity, but we won't be your escort."

"Here's the thing," Amity said. "I've got another job to do, and Galahad is waiting for me at the Canyon Point safehouse in Utah. I'm wanted in the Lower Northeast in less than a fortnight. If you think I can afford detour time on account of your sweaty palms, you're mistaken."

"Your schedule is hardly our problem," Bet started to say, but then Amity interrupted her with a single word, and she fell silent.

"What'd you say?" Leda said softly.

"I said *Galahad,*" Amity replied. "That's my contact in Utah. That's who I answer to. And I don't doubt that's who you answer to. Tell me I'm wrong." Bet's face didn't move, and neither did Leda's, and their stillness was answer enough. "Now," Amity continued, "if you'd like to be the one to tell her that you set me loose in the desert because you were afraid of the big bad sheriff, I welcome you to go on ahead and do it. But my feeling is that none of us wants Galahad feeling stood up at the dance. Do I have that right?"

Bet was still for another moment before she broke. She whipped her hat off and let it slap her thigh hard. "Whiskey-shits," she spat. "Why wouldn't you just tell us? Why'd you have to go ridin' high in front like that? I killed a man yesterday because of you," she added.

"You killed six men yesterday because of me," Amity corrected her. "They needed killing, though, didn't they? What kind of good man becomes a sheriff these days? What kind of good man joins his posse?"

"*Needs* doesn't pay the cost of killing a man," Bet said, and there was a wound in her voice deeper than a bullet could travel. "Just because he needed killing doesn't mean I can sleep easy."

Amity let the weight of that settle over them all before she answered, and when she did, her voice was gentler than it had been before. "I didn't tell you because I was told not to. My instructions were to get to Utah in one piece."

"What about Gen and Trace?" Leda asked, her chin snapping up with sudden realization. "What are they?"

"I wouldn't tell you if they were working the same job as me," Amity replied. "So, I don't know why you'd think to believe me. But for whatever it's worth, they're on the level. They just want a life together, same as they told you."

Bet was still staring at the ground, her jaw working furiously. "Damn," she muttered to herself. "Galahad," she added with the same venom she'd used for the swear.

"Let the girl go," Leda said to Amity, her gaze as cold and flat as gunmetal. "You don't need leverage anymore."

"You ain't sworn yet," Amity replied, all the light drained out of her voice. "Both of you do that, and then I'll turn the pup loose."

Something deep in Esther objected. Hadn't she proven by now that she was more than a pup? But that objection evaporated like spilled water at high noon—she was trapped and trembling, and she sure wasn't about to put up a fight.

Slow and steady, Bet and Leda each drew their revolvers. Esther cringed instinctively away from Amity's gun, sure that she was about to get gutshot, but Amity's iron grip held her steady. "Hush," Amity whispered, even though Esther hadn't made a sound. "You watch, now. You'll want to know how this works." Esther hardly needed the instructions—she couldn't seem to look away from Bet and Leda's hands. Each of them removed a single bullet from the belly of their revolver. "See?" Amity continued. "That bullet in Bet's hand, that's a promise. She's giving it to me, and if she breaks her promise, I'll have a bean in the wheel with her name on it."

Bet and Leda held their hands out, a bullet in each palm. "Go on, then," Bet said.

"Go on," Amity repeated, still whispering in Esther's ear. "My hands are full. You've got to accept this promise for me, pup."

Esther looked back and forth between Bet and Leda, half-numb with fear. Leda caught her eye and nodded, just once, slow and sure.

Esther reached out with trembling fingers and picked up the bullets. Her fingers brushed each woman's palm in turn. Bet's was slick with sweat. Leda's was dry as bone.

"Hop those in my breast pocket," Amity said. Esther did as she was told, reaching awkwardly behind her to deposit the bullets in the pocket of Amity's shirt. "There," Amity said, cheerful as anything. She didn't so much let Esther go as vanish from behind her, so suddenly that Esther staggered at her absence. "Careful, now," Amity added, steadying Esther with a firm hand on her arm.

Bet sighed, rolling her shoulders. "We'll have to tell the others," she said. "No use trying to keep this a secret, I think, and it wouldn't be fair to put them at risk without giving them the chance to turn tail if they need to."

Amity smiled, holstering her revolver. "That's fine," she said, "that's just fine. Let's not make anyone hear this news with a cold belly, though. Leda, I think you've got a bottle of something good tucked away, don't you?"

Leda pursed her lips. "I don't think I do. We can drink out of your stash."

"Fair's fair," Amity replied, still smiling. "Round 'em up, Esther. We've got a heap of discussin' to do."

◦⤳◦

The Bitter Springs checkpoint was the last hurdle the Librarians had to clear before they could get to the safe territory of Utah. The story Bet planned to spin was one that had apparently worked plenty of times before—that they were heading to Marble Canyon to deliver Approved Materials to the tiny outpost there. There was no reason for any suspicion to arise in response to this story—bringing Approved Materials to tiny outposts was the primary reason the Librarians existed. And they would deliver their goods to Marble Canyon, just as promised.

Then they would keep right on, riding their horses to Big Water to meet with the insurrectionists. *With the rebellion,* Esther mentally corrected herself.

The word *insurrectionists* didn't fit right anymore.

The ride to Bitter Springs was a long one, and there wasn't a single thing easy about it. The days were hot and the nights were cold and the wind was high, but not nearly so high as the tension between Amity and everyone else who was stuck riding with her. She'd made her case clear enough, but that hadn't endeared her to a single one of the Librarians. Genevieve and Trace seemed unsure of how they were supposed to feel—they'd known that Amity wasn't who she claimed to be, of course, but they hadn't realized the danger she was putting everyone in by refusing to hide herself away, and they didn't know how much guilt they were supposed to feel. They seemed relieved when, a mile from the checkpoint, Leda told them to get off their horses and hide in the false compartment under the supply wagon.

They weren't alone in their confusion. Nobody seemed to know how much guilt they were supposed to feel, except for Amity, who by all appearances had never been acquainted with remorse in all her days. But everyone else was saddled strange with a combination of resentment and repentance.

Esther would have felt all at sea if she hadn't been surrounded on all sides by desert. Bet and Leda were oddly solicitous in a way that left her dizzy. Amity was as bright and brittle in her friendliness as she had been before she'd jammed a six-gun into Esther's ribs. Cye wouldn't talk to her at all, wouldn't even look at her. Everything was upside-down.

"You know, I meant everything I said," Amity said after a few hours of riding. Her tone was just as light as it had been when she'd been a finger-twitch away from introducing a bullet to Esther's belly. "No hard feelings, not from me."

Esther didn't look over at Amity, or at least she tried not to look. She'd been trying not to look ever since Amity'd let her go. As they'd sat around the campfire getting everyone on the same page, and as they'd finished packing up the wagons, and as they'd tacked up the horses, and as they'd ridden side by side—she'd tried not to look at the woman who had betrayed them all, the woman who had given her a taste of hope.

"I don't know why you think she'd care if you got hard feelings or not," Cye spat. They rode just a little in front of Esther and Amity, right in the center of everyone. From where they sat, they could put eyes on every person in the crew and both wagons, if they'd only turn their head to do it. But, like Esther, they'd been spending the ride staring straight ahead, trying not to set eyes on anything more complicated than the road in front of them.

"Well, you see," Amity drawled, louder than she had to, "we're some kind of friends. We bonded in the desert, is what happened, and now I feel a need to make sure Hopalong here knows we're square, just like I told her before, while you were napping."

The line of Cye's back stiffened. "Don't think there's no hard feelings between us about that 'nap,'" they said. Their hand drifted to the goose egg on the back of their head, where the butt of Amity's revolver had put them to bed before she'd gone to eavesdrop on Esther's confession.

"I'd never worry about hard feelings from you," Amity said easily. "Esther, though. I wouldn't want her as an enemy."

Esther knew that bait was being dangled in front of her. It was almost a relief to take it.

"What's that supposed to mean?" she asked, and even without looking, she could see Amity's catlike mouth curling up at the corners.

"Kind of girl who rides all the way to Endurance on her own? Hell, you didn't break a sweat when I had my smoke-wagon in your side. You're made of something tougher than you look."

Esther couldn't have felt heat rising in her cheeks if she was on fire, not with the sun beating her the way it was, but her heart leapt in a way she couldn't fight. But she couldn't thank Amity.

"That is a hell of a thing for you to say to me," she said, and her voice came out low and husky, in a way she'd only ever heard herself speak when she'd been alone with Beatriz in the dark. "You don't know the half of how tough I am," she added, and even she couldn't tell if she was blowing smoke.

"I think I do," Amity said. "But maybe only half."

Esther bit her cheeks, trying to keep from smiling. She told herself that Amity's approval didn't matter. But it did, and seeing how much the conversation burned Cye's wick didn't hurt, either. Esther broke for just an instant, glancing over at Amity, and she saw the assassin's sidelong smile, and she knew that none of it was an accident.

"You can fuck right off into the Canyon," Esther said, trying to keep the grin out of her voice.

Amity tipped her hat. "I've just been waiting for an invitation," she said. "I'll go let the boss know about it. Wouldn't want to fuck off into the Canyon without giving notice." With that, she clicked her tongue at her horse and trotted past Cye until she was caught up to Bet and Leda.

"She'll just try and charm them, too," Cye muttered.

"Won't work," Esther replied, watching the way Cye's hips rolled with the motion of their horse's back. "She couldn't charm a snake into biting. Bet won't budge an inch for her."

"Hmph." Cye spat, but their heart didn't seem in it. "Charm or none, I hope she's right about you."

"Why's that?" Esther asked, her belly still warm from Amity's conspiratorial smile. That warmth dropped away at Cye's next words, though.

"Because those lights up there? Those are the lookouts for the Bitter Springs checkpoint," they said, gesturing at the tall wooden tower a quarter of a mile ahead. Lights shone off the sides of it, illuminating the road. A lookout post perched at the top of the tower, and Esther shivered at the feel of binoculared eyes watching her from so far away.

"It doesn't look to me like Amity's about to hide away in the wagon," she murmured.

Cye glanced over their shoulder at Esther. Their face was grim, their wide eyes dark with warning. They tipped their hat back off their forehead so they could see Esther clear. "I hope you're ready for another fight, Hopalong," they said. "Because a fight's about to be ready for you."

CHAPTER

10

The bell at the Bitter Springs checkpoint lookout post clanged wildly, the sound of wood hitting brass flat but loud in the still heat of the desert air. As soon as Bet heard the sound, she stuck two fingers in her mouth and let out a piercing whistle, raising her other fist high in the air.

The bell faltered. All of the horses in the Librarians' convoy stopped walking, even Esther's. They knew that whistle, it seemed. So did the guard posted at the lookout.

The air hung heavy after Bet's whistle, and for a long minute, no one moved. Then the door at the foot of the lookout tower opened, and a figure stood silhouetted in the doorway. The bell hadn't started to clang until the convoy was within a hundred feet of passing it—just far enough that Esther couldn't make out the details of the figure's face, but close enough for her to see that he wasn't looking friendly. He stayed put, and after a moment's hesitation, Bet dismounted, handing the reins of her horse over to Leda.

The figure didn't move to greet her. Slowly, Bet began walking toward the tower. She held her hands by her sides—not raising them in the air but keeping them both clearly visible. "Evening, Hooch," she called, her voice steady, aggressively calm.

"Sure is," the man replied flatly, taking a single step past his doorway. Esther wondered if Hooch was his real name. "Where you headed, Bet?"

Bet kept walking toward him at that same slow, careful pace. "Marble Canyon," she said. "Same's always."

Hooch took another step out into the sand. The farther he got from the bright interior of the lookout tower, the easier he was to see. Esther could just make out the bright star on his vest, and her throat tightened, remembering the way blood had found its way into the outline of the eagle on the Sedona sheriff's star.

"Who's that you've got with you?" the lookout asked, lifting his chin. Genevieve and Trace had been hidden away for a mile, and Amity was supposed to have joined them, but of course she hadn't. Something in the set of Leda's shoulders told Esther that she and Bet had accepted this, had accepted the fight it would probably represent.

But Bet acted like a fight was the furthest thing from

her mind. She cocked her head and glanced over her shoulder. "Them?" she said, cool as well water. "Trainees. Me and Leda, we're getting old. Coming up on retirement time for the both of us." She took a few more steps toward Hooch, her every step as loud as a rattling tail.

"You oughta stop there, Bet," Hooch said. He almost sounded regretful.

"Something the matter?" Bet asked in a carrying voice, still walking toward Hooch. Her volume was no accident—something Esther realized only when she saw that Amity and Leda were both resting ready hands on their guns.

"Get ready, Hopalong," Cye muttered.

"I'll need to talk to that trainee of yours," he said. "And the rest of the posse will, too. Stop there, now, don't come any closer."

Cye's palomino took a few steps to one side, tossing its head. Cye clicked their tongue, and the horse came to a halt, flicking its tail nervously.

"She's approved for travel. Do you need to take a look at her papers?" Bet said. She was nearly within reach of the lookout. He glanced over his shoulder, back toward his doorway, shaking his head, but Bet kept closing the distance between them. "I've got 'em right here."

She reached for the inside pocket of her vest. She didn't reach slow.

The lookout noticed.

He shouted something indistinct. He turned to run back into his tower, but in his haste, he tripped over his own feet and sprawled headlong in the dust. Bet fell on him before he could stand up, and the two of them scrapped on the ground for a moment, messy and desperate and grunting. The sun caught on the flat of a knife blade, just a flash of silver in the air and then gone. It was impossible to see who was holding the knife, not in that tangle of limbs. Leda started to get down off her horse, shouting.

The sound of her voice distracted Bet. Just for a moment—but it was a moment too long.

Hooch scrambled out from under her, aiming a clumsy mule-kick behind him. His foot caught her in the temple and then she was on her back, her hat knocked to the ground a few feet behind her. By the time she managed to push herself up onto her elbows, the lookout had slammed the tower door behind him.

Before Leda had gotten to her and helped her to her feet, that brass bell was clanging again, loud and insistent.

"Fuck," Cye spat, watching as Leda and Bet hurried

back toward the convoy. Bet held her hat on her head with one hand, her other hand pressed hard against her rib cage.

"What do we do?" Esther asked. She had only intended for Cye to hear her, but it was Amity who answered.

"You run away, Hopalong," Amity called, a smile in her voice. "Or you stick by. What'll it be?"

A cloud of dust rose, close by and getting closer. Esther could hear hoofbeats. Her lungs suddenly seemed too small to get her enough air. Her horse jerked its head, and she realized she'd been gripping the reins in tight fists. She forced herself to unclench her fingers.

"I'll stick by," she called back.

Soon as she said it, Amity let out a whoop and wheeled her horse around, trotting toward Esther and Cye. Her eyes were lit up bright as a coyote's. "Thought so," she said, grinning wide. "Ain't time to run, anyhow," she added. Her horse pawed at the ground and snorted.

Bet and Leda were back on their horses fast, but it didn't feel fast enough, not while that approaching posse just kept getting closer. "You alright?" Esther called. It felt bold, somehow, shouting up at the Head Librarian, but if there was ever a time to be bold, it was this one. She couldn't hear Bet's reply over the drumbeat of oncoming hooves.

It didn't matter if Bet replied at all. In that moment, it almost didn't matter if Bet was in one piece or not.

There was no more time to talk, no more time to decide.

The posse was on them. The only thing left to do was fight.

∽

Later on, when Esther tried to remember the battle at Bitter Springs, her memory would produce only a few images:

Five men on five coal-black horses. All of the men wore shining silver stars, and all of them were bearing down on the Librarians with rifles drawn and murder in their eyes.

Cye, leaning low over their horse with their teeth bared, charging ahead of Bet and Leda to force the sneering man at the front of the posse off course.

Amity letting out a wild holler before drawing her long-barreled revolver, seeming to aim it at the back of Cye's head, and firing.

At this last, Esther cried out in panic, expecting to see Cye jerk forward into their saddle, their blood spattered across their horse's braided mane. But it wasn't Cye who collapsed in the saddle—it was the man they'd driven off course, the one at the head of the V with the thick black moustache and the hateful snarl. As Cye whooped and Amity gave an answering yell, the man slipped sideways off his horse. Everything was moving too fast for Esther to see the way he hit the ground, and once he was out of sight, the battle began in earnest.

Together, they split the posse in half: Amity and Cye running at the left arm of the V, Bet and Leda running at the right arm. Esther watched, paralyzed. The Librarians' movements were so elegant, so clean, that they looked rehearsed—and Esther had no idea where she might fit in. They drew gunfire away from the wagons, riding through the puffs of dust that went up with each stray bullet. Amity and Leda both had guns drawn, while Bet and Cye rode in complicated circles, keeping the deputies from knowing where to look.

And then, before Esther could decide how to help— before she could even move to join the fray—it was over. Bet and Leda were working together to catch a frothing horse by the reins, and Cye and Amity were dragging a dead man off the back of a black mare.

Esther's belly twisted hard with shame. She hadn't helped. She hadn't done anything. She had sat there on her horse, useless and gawping, waiting to be told what to do as always, just like she'd promised Amity she wouldn't. This time, she'd waited while her traveling companions fought for their lives. They had all been facing an obvious but horrible choice—kill or be killed—and they had all protected each other from that harm. All of them except for her.

Run away or stick by, that's the choice Amity had offered Esther, and she hadn't done either one.

She slid down off her horse, running a hand across its flank. Two completely separate emotions fought for supremacy within her: the need to help *now,* in the aftermath, however she could, battled with overwhelming humiliation at her own uselessness.

You're just in the way here. You're nothing but trouble for anyone, something inside of her whispered in a voice that sounded just like Beatriz. It was a voice she trusted. She slipped into it like an old boot, well-worn and familiar.

She looked back toward the wagon. She loved this life, the long days riding and the cold starry nights and the endless rolling sand and the constant throb in her legs. She loved it because even when someone looked at her with contempt or annoyance or exhaustion, they weren't looking at her with ownership or hate. They were the only people who had told her that it was okay to be who she was. She didn't want to leave.

That doesn't matter, that little Beatriz-voice inside of her whispered. It was reasonable. It was kind. It was a voice that was only trying to protect her, she knew it, and she didn't know how to fight it. *You're only being selfish. You don't belong here.*

Esther lifted her hand to swipe away the hot tears that kept blurring her vision.

It happened fast as a knuckle cracking. Her eyes were only closed for a second—but when she opened them again, lowering her wet hand from her face, she wasn't alone anymore.

A man stood in front of her, his face mottled with blood and dust, the two combining to crust his thick moustache with foul mud. His hair was parted low to one side, and Esther realized that she wasn't looking at the work of a comb, but the work of a bullet—the bullet she'd thought was meant for Cye. The bullet Amity had sent toward this same man with a howl of delight.

The sheriff's deputy had fallen off his horse, but he hadn't stayed down.

The man lunged at Esther, his face contorted with malice, his head still bleeding freely. He swung a fist at her and she threw her arms up in front of her face, trying to remember what Amity had shown her, mixing up the need to dodge with the need to protect her face.

The deputy's fist met with her hands, and the confusion of their limbs kept him from hitting her with the face-breaking force he'd intended. Their hands tangled together for an instant, and at the feel of his callused knuckles, Esther jerked back. Her arms caught his and the momentum of his punch turned into a fall, and then his weight was on her, and her arms were pinned underneath the vast and muscled barrel of his chest, and there was no air, not even enough to scream—and then he rolled away, just enough to get his own arms free.

Just enough for Esther to try to wriggle away.

Just enough for her flailing palm to land on the butt of his revolver.

The gun was still holstered on the deputy's hip, loose and ready to draw, and before Esther could think about what she was doing, there was iron in her hand. She scrambled to her feet, half-skidding away from the deputy. He lifted his hands, palms out, and looked warily at the girl he'd just tried to lay out.

Esther found her footing and stood upright, aiming the man's gun right at his gore-encrusted moustache.

"You don't want to shoot me," he said. It was the first time Esther had heard his voice. It was higher than she expected, cut with a tremor. He was young under all that grime and hate. "I didn't try to shoot you, did I?" He nodded toward the gun in her hand. "Because I knew you were different from them. I could have tried to shoot you, but I didn't because you're not like those other ones. You would never kill a man," he added, and he sounded more confident this time. "Not you. You're better than they are. You're not a killer, sweetheart."

Esther's finger rested alongside the trigger. He was right—she didn't want to shoot him—but she didn't see how she had a choice in the matter. She didn't relish being called "sweetheart," but something deep in her chimed at the word: this was a man who would let her go, if she was nice and pliant and didn't cause trouble. This was a man who wanted her to be the kind of woman who liked to hear "sweetheart," and that was a role she knew how to play.

She could escape, safe. She could go back to a life of hiding who she was, playing the role assigned to her. She could do it if she wanted to.

But she wasn't sure she wanted to.

"I can't let you go," she said. "I can't let you tell anyone what happened here today."

"I won't tell them about *you*," he said, and he sounded so reasonable that it was almost easy to forget what that promise meant for Cye and Bet and Leda, for the Librarians and the work they did, for the only people Esther had ever met who were like her and liked themselves for it. "You're not like them," he repeated, his eyes softening, his hands starting to drop to his sides. "They're not good people. You must know that."

Esther's head swam, because he still wasn't wrong.

The Librarians were road-hardened and cutthroat. They were killers, Amity especially. They had done all of this before, there could be no doubt about that, and there could be no doubt that they would do it again.

Esther would tell herself later that she hadn't been about to let the deputy run off, but when she was frank with herself, late at night with the stars to keep her honest, she couldn't be sure what she'd been about to do.

All she could be sure of was that Trace made the decision for her. The back flap of the supply wagon lifted, and Trace's shock of red hair spilled out of it. She was facing away from Esther and the deputy at first, obviously checking to see if the coast was clear. When she turned around to look at them, her mouth widened into an O of shock.

Esther and the deputy were both distracted, just for a moment, but the deputy recovered faster than Esther could. He lunged again, grabbing for the gun. In that moment, Esther knew clear as the blue desert sky that the deputy would kill her. He would kill Genevieve and Trace too, and Bet and Leda and Cye and everyone like them. Even if he didn't do the job with his own hands, he would be the instrument of their deaths. She knew that he would see to it that they swung just the same as Beatriz had, or that they lined up against a wall to take as many bullets as a firing squad could put in them. It didn't matter to him if they were good people or bad people, if they were goat farmers or assassins. It didn't matter to him, just the same as it hadn't mattered to Esther's own father.

He would kill them all, because that's what the State told him was right, and because the State told him he was important for doing it.

Esther lifted the gun and sighted down the barrel just the way she'd seen Amity do it, and she pulled the hammer back, and she tightened her grip on the trigger until it snapped under her finger.

The gun kicked up high, whipping back toward her, but she caught herself before she fell and held herself steady enough to cock the hammer and fire again, and again, and again until the trigger was clicking and her ears were ringing and the deputy was sprawled motionless in the dust.

She couldn't look away from him, not even after Cye eased the spent revolver out of her fingers, not even after they pressed their hands to her shoulder and tried to walk her away from the body. She stared over her shoulder at the place where his blood was draining into the desert soil, and she forced herself to memorize what he looked like.

She had seen a man decide that she deserved to die, and she had killed him for it.

The Librarians didn't make it to Marble Canyon after all.

The ride to Big Water was a blur. Esther barely realized that she was on her horse, not until her horse spooked away from a cactus that looked just the same as every other cactus along the trail. She startled when her horse did, jerking at the reins for a moment before forcing herself to calm down enough to soothe the horse.

"There you are." Cye's voice came from Esther's left, gentler than Esther had ever heard them. "You back with us now?"

Esther shook her head. "Not sure," she admitted. "How long have we been riding?"

"Few hours," Cye said. "We'll be at Big Water by sundown."

The sun was already slung low in the sky. Even without that evidence, Esther would have believed that she'd been riding for hours because her mouth was too dry even to taste foul. That changed once she drained half her canteen, and she spat to try to get the sour off her tongue. She took another sip of water, trying to figure out what it was she needed to ask Cye. "What . . ." she started, but she didn't have the words to follow it.

"We had to get out of there," Cye said, answering the question Esther hadn't been able to form: *what happened between then and now?* "We were already packed, so it was just a matter of getting you on your horse. Sorry we didn't have time to clean you up," Cye added, and for the first time, they looked at Esther, their mouth tight with apology.

"What's—oh," Esther said, looking down at her hands and actually seeing them this time. She was covered in dust, hands and arms both, and she was willing to bet that the rest of her looked just as filthy. Her knuckles and wrists and elbows were skinned up, and she remembered with startling clarity the feeling of being trapped between the sandy gravel and the deputy who had fallen onto her. She lifted her fingers to her face—both were half-numb, but she could feel a distant sting when she touched her cheek and her lower lip.

"Yeah," Cye said. "You're pretty banged up. Not as bad as you oughta be, though, taking that Clydesdale on by yourself." They grimaced. "Not as bad as Bet's banged up. Be thankful for that."

Esther looked sharply at Cye, then at the rest of the convoy. Everything came into focus a few seconds too slowly. Esther wondered if she'd hit her head, if something was wrong with her. "Where's Bet?" she asked, her stomach filling with cold dread, because she was sure she knew the answer. *You did this,* that voice inside her whispered. *You spread your poison on these people, and now Bet's dead too.* The voice didn't seem so reasonable anymore. It almost seemed cruel.

It sounded less like Beatriz than it ever had.

"She's in the supply wagon," Cye said. Then, seeing Esther's face, they quickly added: "She's alive, don't worry, she's—aw, hell, Hopalong, don't cry—"

But Esther wasn't crying. Her face crumpled, sure, and her throat clenched—and she leaned off the side of her horse to vomit onto the trail. Her stomach felt like a fist. All the water she'd swallowed came back up out of her, splashing into the sand, gone as fast as it landed.

Amity's laugh cut through the air from behind them, fast and sharp as the bullet that had grazed that deputy. She clapped, and the sound made Esther's stomach draw in on itself again.

"Sorry," Cye said, handing over their own canteen. "Take little sips. I should have told you."

"Bet's alive?" Esther choked out. She poured Cye's

water into her mouth from high up, just enough to rinse the taste of bile from her throat.

"More than," Cye said. "Drink the rest of that, I've got another. But take your time, Hopalong. Your belly thinks you're still in the fight. It'll huck up ballast."

"Seems you spend all your time teaching me how to drink water," Esther said, allowing herself a small smile.

Cye laughed. They sounded relieved. "Suppose I do," they said. "Listen," they went on, their voice dropping a little lower, a little more somber. "Bet's alive, and she's mad as hell—not at you," they added. "That lookout caught her between the ribs. The knife was a little old thing, but it got her bad, and she's no good for the road, not for at least a month. That's what Amity said, anyway."

Esther couldn't be sure if Amity had been eavesdropping the whole time, or if she heard her name and decided that was her cue to butt in. "I was right to say it too," she said, trotting up between Esther and Cye as if there was enough room for her. "How're you feeling, bruiser?"

Esther shook her head. "Don't call me that," she said. "I let you two down. I didn't do anything worth—"

"You sure did," Amity interrupted. "Look at yourself, girl. I would say to look at that deputy, but . . ." One corner of her mouth curved into something that looked like a smile but felt like a frown. "I'm sorry, Esther," she added, some of the brass sanded off her tone. "I thought he was down. If I'd known he wasn't—"

"I shouldn't have left you alone," Cye said, their voice rough at the edges. "I shouldn't have left you behind like that. I knew you weren't behind me, and I just left you there."

"He's dead, isn't he?" Esther asked in a whisper. She knew the question was stupid—she'd put six bullets into the man, at a close-enough range that she could see the surprise in his eyes when the first one hit him. But she needed to hear it.

"Dead as shoe leather, and fixing to stay that way," Amity said.

Esther shook her head. "I should feel worse about it," she said. "Shouldn't I?"

"You will," Amity answered. "Sit tight. It'll come get you later, when you're trying to sleep, when you're trying to eat. But I'll tell you for free that you did the only thing you could have done." She flicked her horse's reins, picking up speed to leave Cye and Esther behind. "You did right," she called over her shoulder.

"Sorry about her," Cye said. "She's not one of ours, you know? People who do her kind of work—I think they have to harden up to do it without breaking."

Esther took a small sip of water, stopping herself from gulping at the canteen. "I can't decide if I want to harden up or not," she said. "It seems awful nice from where I'm sitting."

Cye looked at Esther sidelong. "I don't want you to," they said. "I like you better how you are."

Heat flooded Esther's throat and belly. That sidelong glance, that almost-smile, *I like you better*—it was enough to make her fingers twitch on the canteen. She almost couldn't believe herself. Now, of all times, so soon after she'd killed a man, how could she be feeling anything but monstrous? But there it was, that flush that Cye brought out of her. "You like me?"

"Don't tell nobody," Cye said wryly. "But yeah, I do. I think you've got a good head on your shoulders. You learn fast and you don't give up easy." They nodded as though they were considering their own words. "I like you fine, Hopalong. I think you'll do us credit on the road."

Esther's head swam. She couldn't tell if Cye was saying what it sounded like they were saying. She couldn't even tell exactly what it sounded like they were saying. Was she being allowed to stay? Would she get to be a Librarian?

Did Cye like her as a friend, or as a colleague, or as something else, something deeper and more urgent and more impossible?

She didn't get a chance to find out anything more.

The sun dipped behind the horizon, and Amity's sharp whistle pierced the dusk. An answering whistle sounded from close by, and several shapes detached themselves from the desert, approaching the convoy.

They'd reached the Big Water outpost, which could only mean one thing.

They were among the insurrectionists.

They were among the rebels.

They were safe.

Cye hadn't exaggerated about Bet being angry. She was mad as a mountain cat. Moving her from the supply wagon to the kitchen table at the Big Water doctor's house made her bleed fresh, and the pain made her spit a string of profanities so poisonous that even Leda blanched.

"I think she'll live," the doctor drawled by way of a greeting, pulling on a pair of latex gloves.

Esther stared, open-mouthed. "Where did you get those?" she asked before she could stop herself.

"Who's this?" the doctor asked Leda. His tone was mild, but Esther caught the suspicious glint in his eye, and she remembered that she was an outsider here.

"She's fine," Leda said. "Apprentice-level clearance."

The doctor nodded, satisfied, and Esther wondered what *Apprentice-level* meant. Leda hadn't just called her an Apprentice and left it at that—but *clearance* had to mean something, didn't it? Her hopes rose just enough that she felt them fall when Leda added, "She's seen everything we'd let a trainee see, anyhow."

"These gloves are military-issue," the doctor told Esther, beginning to cut through Bet's shirt with a pair of curved shears. He said it as though it answered her question.

"Save this shirt once you're done mangling it," Bet growled. "The buttons are still good, at least."

"Hush," the doctor snapped, and Bet closed her mouth with visible resentment.

With that, Leda stepped between Esther and the scene on the kitchen table. "Enough for now," she said, laying a firm but gentle hand on Esther's shoulder. "You don't need to see her getting stitched up, and she don't need you watching it." Esther nodded, starting to feel ashamed—why hadn't she left soon as Bet was set down on the table?—but then Leda gave her shoulder a squeeze and added, "Thanks for trying to stick by, though. It's friendly of you."

Esther nodded again and left the doctor's kitchen, walking out into the dusty little yard where Cye and

Amity were waiting. The sky was filled with stars, and candlelight filled the windows of the dozen houses that composed the town of Big Water.

"Where's Gen and Trace?" she asked, at the same time as Cye asked, "How bad's Bet look?"

"They're watering the horses," Cye answered.

"Not so bad," Esther replied, and Cye let out a hard breath, their shoulders dropping. "She's still cussing hot murder," she added.

"That's good news," Amity said. "So, what's eating at you? Don't look at me like I'm a talking mule, girl. There's something stuck in your teeth. What is it?"

"That doctor," Esther said after a moment. "He has latex gloves. And I saw a generator in his kitchen, which means he has diesel. But I know he's not collecting rations, and even if he was, rations wouldn't cover gloves like that. Even the doctor in Valor couldn't get hold of those things—he had to dunk his hands in corn whiskey and boiling water before pulling out my bad tooth last year. So . . ."

"Ah." Amity nodded. "Wondered when you'd get here. Do you know what the Librarians do?"

"Don't," Cye said softly, but Amity ignored her.

"They deliver Approved Materials," Amity said. "And they deliver people, like me and like Gen and like Trace.

And they deliver gloves." Amity gave Esther a hard look, one that asked how smart she was and how much she was willing to understand.

Esther stared back, and all of it fell together. Why there would be a secret compartment in the bottom of the supply wagon, and why Bet and Leda had been so furious to find her hiding in that same wagon, so close to everything they were hiding even before they'd picked up their parcel. Why Cye hadn't wanted her to help put away those fabric parcels outside Town, the parcels she'd assumed held nothing more forbidden than fresh-baked bread. Why the possession of Unapproved Materials would be a hanging offense.

What Beatriz had been up to before she died.

"They pick up supplies in the towns they go to," she said slowly, and Amity's eyes sparkled with approval. "And they bring them here? But that would mean that there are people—"

"Everywhere," Cye murmured. They were watching Esther just as intently as Amity was, their face still, their dimples nowhere to be seen. "There are cells in all the major cities, and people working on their own in every town. Hell, people in the major cities too, who think they're on their own."

People like Beatriz. That's what she meant—people like Beatriz, who had known there was another life somewhere out there, and people like Esther, who hadn't. Esther wondered, then, if Beatriz had been planning to tell her that they weren't the only ones.

"Everywhere," Esther whispered to herself. "There are people like us everywhere."

Cye and Amity looked at each other, then back at Esther. "Yeah, Hopalong," Cye said carefully. "People like us."

CHAPTER
12

Esther didn't realize what she'd said until she heard it coming out of Cye's mouth. She looked up, alarmed, hoping she hadn't overstepped, hoping she hadn't overplayed her hand. Hoping she was allowed to use that word—*us*.

The kitchen door opened behind her, and Leda stepped out. She leaned against the outer wall of the house, letting out a long, slow sigh. "She's fine," she said. "Spitting mad but fine. She won't be able to sit a horse for six weeks, so she'll be a bigger pain in my side than that knife was in hers, but we'll get back to it after a stretch."

Amity shook her head, her arms folded. "Don't think you will, Leda," she said, her mouth hitched in that same frown of a smile.

"What's that supposed to mean?" Leda asked sharply, and Amity lifted her hands in surrender.

"Whoa, there," she said. "I just mean, you two don't want to get on that road again. Ask Bet—I'm sure she saw the same thing I did."

"And what the hell is it you think you saw?" Leda snapped.

Amity folded her arms again, cooling off fast as the desert sand when the sun goes down. "She got made."

Those three words took all the air out of Leda's anger. She leaned back against the wall again, deflated, and pressed the heels of her hands to her eyes. "Fuck," she hissed. "You're right."

"That lookout wasn't waiting for me," Amity said. "I mean—he was, but he was also waiting for Bet. And that posse was ready and waiting," she added. "She's been made for sure. Word spread, Leda. It was only a matter of time."

Leda shook her head, still covering her eyes. "God-damn it," she said again. "Shit, fuck, hellfire—"

"Yep," Amity agreed. Cye and Esther looked to each other, both aware that this conversation was above their understanding, both aware that the news was bad.

"Alright," Leda said at last. "Alright. Fine." She shook her head. "She's asleep right now, and she sore needs it," she said. She leveled a hard glare at Amity, then turned it on Cye and Esther. "None of you three tell her a damn thing. Let me give her the news. She'll be ready to do a murder once she finds out I already cleared it with Galahad."

Amity flashed her teeth at Leda, not anything that could quite be called a smile. "Don't you worry about that," she said. "I intend to be a night's ride from here when you tell her." She turned to Esther and Cye and gave them a wink. "Good luck with that blue streak she'll be aiming at all of you," she said.

With that, she stuck her hands into her pockets and walked into the night.

"I think that was as much of a 'goodbye' as she knows how to give," Cye muttered.

"Good riddance," Leda answered.

"I don't know," Esther said. "I thought she was nice."

Leda and Cye stared at Esther, more incredulous than they'd been when Amity had pronounced that Bet wouldn't be traveling anymore. Esther shrugged at them, trying not to feel the embarrassment that came with being looked at like she'd sprouted hooves. She meant what she'd said—for all that Amity had taken her hostage, for all her wry cruelty, for all the blood on her hands . . . she was still the first person who'd really made Esther feel like things might turn out alright in the end.

"You're traumatized, Hopalong," Cye finally said.

They draped an arm across Esther's shoulders. "Traumatized and exhausted. You'll think straight in the morning."

"I don't think I will," Esther said—but she let Cye lead her to the wagons, where Genevieve and Trace had watered the horses and laid out the bedrolls. The warm weight of Cye's arm across her shoulders stayed with her as she stretched out on the ground. It turned out that they had been right about the exhaustion. Esther fell asleep before she could even begin to marvel at the stars that filled the desert sky, before she could begin to relive the fighting and the killing, before she could begin to worry about tomorrow.

❧

Esther would never know how Bet reacted when she heard the news of her retirement. She would never know what became of Amity, either—although she never again heard news about the death of anyone in a position of power without wondering if they'd seen that glint-eyed grin of hers in their last moments.

She spent a couple of days camped out with Cye and Genevieve and Trace just outside Big Water. She brushed the horses and kept them fed, and she cleaned tack and beat out bedrolls. She worked hard, and it was all work that needed doing, but she and Cye both knew what she was really up to.

She was waiting.

At the end of that third day, Leda came out to the camp to fetch them. "You two've got a job to do," she said.

She brought Esther and Cye to Bet's bedside in the back of the doctor's house. It was a simple room, clean, and it had machines in it that Esther had only ever seen in the Why We Fight reels that played before Approved movies—the kinds of machines a brave soldier gunned down in battle might be hooked up to. The machines were quiet now, but Esther knew that if the doctor's generator ran, they could beep and hiss and somehow, they could keep a person alive.

Bet looked exactly like herself. She was propped up in the bed, her back against an absurdity of pillows. Her shirt hung loose on her frame, as though she'd shrunk inside of it, but her eyes were bright and her shoulders were straight, and she looked ready to parley.

"So," she said when Cye and Esther entered the room. "You two ready to work?"

"Sure thing, boss," Cye said.

Esther nodded, not sure if she would be able to speak, but that nod wasn't good enough.

"You'd best be able to answer me if you think you want this job," Bet snapped.

"Yes, ma'am," Esther said. "Yes, I'm ready to work."

"Are you sure?" Bet asked, her voice a little gentler. "You're alright after Bitter Springs?"

Esther hesitated before answering. It would have been easy to lie—easy to say yes, to say whatever it took to become a real Librarian. But she felt like maybe she was done with lying, and she decided to try on the truth instead. "No," she said. "I'm not alright and I don't know that I'll ever be alright. But I still want the job. Amity told me—" She hesitated again, not wanting to give away too much, but Bet's eyes were locked on hers and they drew the rest out of her. "Amity told me that there's more like us. Everywhere, all over." Bet nodded at this, and Esther went on, the words coming to her just an instant after the things she'd been feeling solidified into ideas that words could even describe. "If there's more like us, and if everywhere the State controls is the same . . . then I'd bet they're just as scared as I've always been. I'd bet they're just as hopeless." She shook her head, looked down at her hands. "That's not right. And if we can help make that stop, then I'm okay with not being alright."

Bet gave another nod, this one firm and final.

"Good," she said. "Because you two are in charge of the Library now."

Cye's shock was even more obvious than Esther's. "What?" they cried, their hands lifting in some aborted gesture of bewilderment. "But we can't— We're not ready, we don't know how to—"

"Sure you do," Leda said easily from the opposite side of Bet's bed. "You know as much as we could teach you, anyhow. And you can teach your little Hopalong here as much as we would have taught her."

"But I'm just an apprentice," Cye whispered in anguish.

Bet and Leda smiled twin cat-grins. "You're no such thing," Bet said. She reached into her shirt pocket and drew out the shining Head Librarian badge she'd been wearing when she discovered Esther in the back of the supply wagon just a few weeks before. She held it out to Cye, who stared at it, their face blank with terror.

"You can do this, Cye," Leda said. "You're the Head Librarian now. You have to be," she added, nodding at Esther. "Can't have an Assistant Librarian without a Head Librarian."

Cye took the badge gingerly, holding it in their palm like a tarantula. "What's the job?" they asked, their voice distant.

"You two need to get Genevieve and Trace to Provo,"

Bet said, all business now. She outlined the route they'd need to take, the dangers they'd face, the safehouses they could afford to stop at on the way. "It'll only take a few days if you do it right," she said, "but I won't start to worry until you've been gone a fortnight."

By the time Cye and Esther left the doctor's house, both their heads were swimming. Leda walked them out, stopping them just outside the door.

"I'm going to give you some advice," she said. "You might not like it, but you're getting it anyway." Cye and Esther waited, and Leda looked them over, considering them as thoroughly as if they were her equals. "Give it a year," she said.

"What?" Cye asked.

"Give it a year before you decide you're not cut out for it," she replied. "That's how long it'll take you to trust each other. That's how long it'll take you to feel like you've got the hang of the road, like you're not lost. Don't give up before then, and you won't give up after." Cye nodded, and after a moment, they stuck out their hand. Leda shook it. "Now, get along," she said. "You'll need to pack up tonight if you want to get on the road to Provo by morning."

"Thank you," Esther said, wishing there were stronger words than those. "I won't let you down."

"'Course you will," Leda replied, smiling. "But you'll

try your hardest not to, and that's worth more than a promise."

She disappeared into the house, leaving Cye and Esther to stare at each other in abject shock. "You're an Assistant Librarian," Cye whispered to Esther, a slow, deep-dimpled smile spreading across their face.

"And you're a Head Librarian," Esther replied, biting her lip hard to keep from matching that smile with one of her own.

Cye grabbed her by the wrist and ran with her toward camp, holding their hat on their head with the other hand. Esther stumbled behind them, tripping over her own feet as she tried to keep up, kicking up dust behind her. Cye looked back, a wild glint in their eyes, then stopped running.

"This is far enough," they panted.

"Far enough for what?" Esther gasped back.

"Far enough for nobody to hear this," Cye said, and then their arms were around Esther's waist, tight and strong and sure. "Head Librarian!" They shouted as they lifted Esther into the air, her knees knocking into their belt. They let out a loud whoop as they spun her around fast and sudden. *"Head Librarian!"* They shouted their new title again, and Esther couldn't do a thing to stop the laugh that rose up out of her, and she couldn't do a thing to stop herself from whooping right back.

"Put me down!" she laughed, gripping Cye's strong shoulder in one hand and holding her hat down with the other, wanting nothing less than to be put down—but Cye did what she asked for, not what she wanted, and just like that, Esther's feet were back on the ground.

But Cye's arms were still around her, and they weren't letting go.

Esther's nose nearly touched theirs. That glint hadn't left their eyes, not one bit—if anything, it was getting brighter the longer they looked at Esther, the longer they hung on to her waist. Their gaze dropped to her mouth, and their fingers flexed at the small of her back, and she hoped, and she wanted, and she needed—

And then they were kissing her. Sudden and certain, just like everything else they did. They held her waist firm, and she stayed as put as put can be because she couldn't think of a single other place she'd rather be. Their breath was sweet and their tongue was hot against hers, and the sweat in their hair was cool under her palms. Esther couldn't have said when both of their hats got knocked off, but she didn't miss the hats one bit, the hats could go split logs for all she cared. Who needed hats when Cye's lower lip fit so perfectly between her teeth, when they were pressed so close to her that clothes felt like a joke, when they were laughing softly into her mouth in a way that made Esther think they thought that joke was funny, too?

When they pulled away, they were grinning that broad, easy grin again. They dropped a kiss onto Esther's nose before stooping to pick up their hat.

"Come on, then, Hopalong," they said. "Enough celebrating. We've got a lot of work to do before sundown."

᭖

The next morning, Cye met with Galahad. Esther wasn't invited to the meeting, but she watched as Cye scrubbed their face and neck with a damp rag beforehand, and she saw the stunned smile on their face when they came back to the wagons after, and she supposed that whoever Galahad was, they must have been worth the fuss.

Cye and Esther led the convoy away from Big Water, driving north toward Provo. Genevieve and Trace rode behind them, within sight but not within hearing. Cye glanced over at Esther once every few seconds, and Esther glanced back.

"What is it?" she asked. "You wondering what problems I'll give you between here and Provo?"

"Actually," Cye replied, their dimples deepening, "I'm wondering what we're going to eat for dinner. You never did make that stew you promised, with the wine in it."

Esther leaned back in the saddle to let the early-morning sun catch her face. "Don't suppose you thought to bring any spices other than salt with you?"

Cye squinted at her sideways. "Don't suppose *you* thought to *check*?"

Esther didn't answer, because Cye was right: she hadn't thought to check. She had a lot to learn about life on the road, and she knew it. She also knew that she would have to try to figure things with Cye out sooner or later—the heat that came with their wry glances, the hunger that seemed to simmer below the surface of everything they did. She didn't know how she felt about Cye, didn't know how Cye felt about her. She didn't know if that kiss had been a celebration, or a mistake, or a promise of more.

She thought she wanted it to be a promise of more. She thought about *more* a lot. She couldn't seem to *stop* thinking about *more*.

She would have to figure all that out. Later.

For now, she was just happy to be on the road. She was happy to be a Librarian, even if she was only an Assistant, even if Cye had quietly told her that she was mostly going to function as an Apprentice until she had the hang of things. She was happy to be in danger, because that danger came with a purpose, and she knew exactly what she wanted to do.

She wanted to meet them. Every person in every cell across the Southwest. Every person who came to their camp in the night with supplies or with letters or with fear in their hearts. Everyone who was living the way she had lived up until the night she hid herself in the back of the Librarians' supply wagon—everyone who was sure that there was nothing good in the world for them to have.

She wanted to meet them, and she wanted to tell them the truth that was blooming inside of her, that had been growing bigger and brighter and more certain since she'd first laid eyes on the business end of Bet's revolver. It was a truth that had become more powerful than that little voice, the one that had felt like Beatriz, the one that had felt like safety for so long. It was a truth that didn't feel anything like safety.

It felt better than safety.

It felt like gunpowder at her back, driving her toward a fight that needed winning.

Keep fighting. It will be hard, and it will be awful, and it will be worth it. Don't give up, even when it feels like dying. Don't give up.

This is only the beginning.

Riding toward the horizon, she knew that was the

truth: it was only the beginning. And whatever came next, whatever fight was getting ready for her on the other side of that horizon, she was going to be ready for it. They all would—everyone in every cell across the sector, in every city and every town, in every lonesome shotgun shack, in every jailhouse and every church. They'd all be ready to fight.

The Librarians would make sure of it.

ACKNOWLEDGMENTS

I owe an immense debt of gratitude to the team that made this book possible:

DongWon Song, my brilliant agent;

Ruoxi Chen, my phenomenal editor;

the entire team at Tor.com Publishing, who threw their support behind this book and continue to dazzle me with their dedication to the kind of literature I and so many members of my community are hungry for;

Other Sarah and Elisabeth and Carrie and Sharon and Mallory and Ace and Mark and Jeeyon and Stacey and Adam and Roxy and Mom and Dad and Rachel and Katie, for reading and listening and checking to see that I was still alive when the writing got hard;

the PQ'rs and the MFs and the Slack brigade, and the group text and the group chat, for keeping me sane;

Tinkerbell, for being a very good dog;

Buttercup, for being a very bad cat;

Ryan and Christina, for holding my heart.

∽⌒∂

I also owe this book and my life to my queer community:

The people who saw me when I was struggling with the feeling that I was destined for tragedy; the people who saw me when I was hurting other members of our queer family, and told me so.

The people who took me aside to ask if I was okay, and who took me aside to tell me I was wrong.

The people who reminded me not to abandon myself for the sake of avoiding a fight.

The people who fought for me, in the past and in the present. The people who fought for us. The people who will fight.

I owe this book to all of them, and I owe it to every queer person out there who thinks they don't have a future, who thinks there's no place for them in this world, who thinks that all is lost if they can't find a way to bury the person who they are:

This is for you. This is for all of you. There's a place for you in the future, and it's better than you can possibly imagine.

Please be there to meet it. We need you on our side.